In a world that has become rather bifurcated by digitization, we too easily forget that some of the most interesting material lies in the areas in between. Jønathan Lyons bravely explores these areas in his writing. In one story he writes about the difficulty in choosing the correct pronoun with which to raise an intergender child. In another he writes in words that cancel themselves as they go, just as a family's do. In another he writes about a man who changes his name to a typeface and then to punctuation marks. Lyons realizes that what lies between the dichotomy of "you" and "me" is language, and his playful but serious stories about the challenges and joys of crossing this bridge are both provocative and joyous. I cannot help but think that this is a very important book that I will return to again and again as a reminder of why we have this bridge in the first place.

— Eckhard Gerdes, author of *White Bungalows*.

With much gratitude and thanks to Dominic Ward and Dirt Heart Pharmacy Press for their help in bringing this collection to fruition.

The White Noise Album

Jonathan Lyons

Cicatrix Publications
A Publisher of Experimentation

Lewisburg, PA Windsor, CT

Track List

"Suffer the Children," published in the Dirt Heart
Pharmacy Press anthology, The 8th Madness, 2015.

"Minnows," in Writing that Risks: New Work from
Beyond the Mainstream, Red Bridge Press, July 2013.

"The Good Life," *Phoebe – A Journal of Literature and Arts*,
Vol 36, Issue 1, Spring 2007.

"\-/: The Helvetica Story," *Eleven-Eleven*, Issue 15,
August 2013.

"the reflecting pool," *Hotel Amerika Issue 8.1*, Fall 2009.

"32 Ft/Sec²," *Journal of Experimental Fiction*, Issue 39,
January 2011.

"Calling," *Gargoyle* literary journal, Issue 62, November
2014.

"Waterloo Talking," *Rivet: The Journal of Writing that
Risks*, Issue 1, Summer 2014.

"Signal to Noise (excerpt)," *The Loudest Guffaw*, Vol. 1,
Issue 1, Spring 2007

"Writing the Review," *Pank*, Issue 4, January 2010.

"the gravity of the moment," *Rampike*, November 2008. [Deleted]

"Dashiell," *Gargoyle* literary journal, Issue 83, November
2008

Suffer the Children

To be included in the upcoming Dirt Heart Pharmacy Press anthology.

Now.1

Ne slumps sullenly in nir chair, the gag firmly in place. I will have only a moment to escape the room before ne dooms me with a word — even some small vocalization. But Sasha is my child, my own flesh and blood, and I will not let nir starve. I change nir soiled diaper, then set the plate of steaming food before nir and ready myself to flee.

And I think, *My God, ne's only nine.*

I slip my key into the mechanism on the rear of the gag, but hold the device itself in place.

Maybe I'll get lucky. Maybe ne won't try to speak to me.

Remember, I whisper, trying to sound soothing, *no words. Use the pen and pad.*

I let go of the gag and sprint for the door.

Pa — ne gets out. The blow pounds me into the wall. I cannot breathe; ne's knocked the wind out of me. I struggle through the door, shoving aside my shabby improvisational soundproofing: layers of towels and blankets duct-taped to the door, inside and out. The soundproofing was an impotent effort, though, like so many where my child is concerned.

As my breath slowly begins to return, I wonder what my child was trying to say to me.

Please?

No — *Papa.* My heart, so crumpled from all of this, implodes further. I clutch to my heart the locket Anna gave me at an earlier, happier time. Inside, anachronistically enough, is a small lock of her hair.

My baby, my child; ne just wanted some small comfort from me. Ne meant no harm, but, of course ...

We could not seem to convince nir not to speak. No modes of communication worked efficiently, as without the full range of motion, nir hands could barely — and then, clumsily — use sign language, and writing on a notepad was slow, tedious. I did not blame her. Nir situation, one of rare communication, one of imprisonment, was inhumane. It was all we'd been able to come up with.

I told myself we would only need to keep nir bound and gagged until nir weaponized words faded. This, I hoped, would arrive with adolescence and the radical alterations that brings.

Fracture

When ne was born, our child turned out to be a rare creature: A fully hermaphroditic baby.

The delivery physician told us that it was customary to select a sex for children born between genders and for a surgical team to tailor a child to that decision. I was all for this solution, but Anna would have none of it. A stalwart believer in one's right to self-determination, she demanded that our firstborn be allowed to choose whatever path s/he wanted. But I'd wanted a son, and she was keeping me from having one, and in I resented her for that, and that resentment took hold, and a fracture formed between us.

Anna took on the tasks of choosing a gender-neutral pronoun set, which we integrated into our vocabularies so that we might avoid awkward constructions such as *s/he*. According to ta go-to Web source dedicated to the issue[1]:

> 1. Ne/nem/nir/nirs/nemself
> Ease of pronunciation: 4/5
> Distinction from other pronouns: 4/5
> Gender neutrality: 4.5/5
> Although relatively obscure, this has become my favorite contender. It follows the formats of existing pronouns while staying more gender-neutral than any but Spivak – you could call it gender-balanced. "Ne" is **n**+(he or she), "nem" is **n**+her+**him**, "nir" is**n**+him+her. Because it has a different form for each declension, it doesn't lean towards following male or female patterns – patterns made very obvious when you read works about obviously male characters with female-patterned pronoun forms. The letter "n" itself can stand for "neutral" – a property we are searching for. A reader may be uncertain how to pronounce "ne" at first glance, but pronunciation of the other forms is relatively obvious. One problem when reading aloud is that the "n" sometimes blends with words ending in "n" or "m," but it didn't occur as often and wasn't as problematic as "zir" with words ending in an "s" or "z" sound.

Anna decides to name nir Sasha, a German name for males, but one that's often assigned to female babies in the West.

Before.1

---

[1] https://genderneutralpronoun.wordpress.com/

Sasha and I will head to the park. Anna, who has been noticeably distant from me these past weeks, is booked in a meeting for another hour and a half.

We are fortunate to have a company that specializes in playground equipment calling our tiny town its home: Our parks are exquisitely decked out.

The day is cool, but not cold. The leaves scrape white noise across the pavement, electric in the unforgiving autumn glare. Before this day, I never suspected that the sun might have a mean streak.

Sasha and I chase across the collage of slides and ladders and gangways that our benefactor corporation has designed to resemble a pirate ship. We've brought along a bag of our own, as well, bearing a soccer ball, wiffle ball and bat, even a spongy football. As we head down a high, bumpy slide, ne sprints to our sack and retrieves the soccer ball.

"Catch!" ne yells, beaming. Ne drops the ball and gives it a hell of a kick. It sails over my head and across the park, toward the borough's Main Street. Sasha decides to make it a race. We tear across the grass, and I let my pace flag a bit so ne can beat me to it, when I notice, in the front window of the coffee shop across the way, Anna.

She is not alone. She has an expression of delight on her face that I have not witnessed in ages; her posture is relaxed. Sitting across from her at the small table, a fit, and younger-looking man smiles charmingly and holds her gaze. Their hands touch, then surreptitiously flit apart. Underneath the table, their feet and legs caress one another. I touch the locket again, almost a reflex, as the organs within my chest hammer. The lock of her hair comes from a happier time, a time when an extramarital relationship would have been unthinkable. Realizing who he is sinks my heart like a stone.

These are pleasures missing from my life these long months, and she is gifting them to another man. And not just any other man. All at once, I realize that my Sasha sees all of this, as well — sees nir mother clearly enjoying a romantic moment with nir uncle, my twin brother, Owen. My parents named me, phonetically, the opposite: I am called Noah.

Perhaps he reminds Anna of who and what I used to be. He is more in-shape than I am, and the effect does render him seemingly younger than me. I cannot deny that I've put on a few pounds, and that working out has never been my thing. I've let myself slide. I'm a lump.

My child stares for a time at nir mother and nir uncle, nir face burning with fury at Anna. Then nir gaze turns to me. Ne is imploring me to interrupt, to acknowledge what we are witnessing, to *do something*. But I find myself immobile, terrified of what I am seeing, completely bereft of the will to act.

I pick up the ball and tell my child that it is time to go home.

Nir expression of fury and alarm, that look of desperation for me to *do something* to set things right before our world breaks, undergoes a slow transmogrification. My child cannot accept nir ineffectual, impotent father, nor his failure to take even a single, minimal step to preserve their family, their world. Everything is about to shatter.

Now.2

When the first reports of this began to appear, we regarded it as a hoax, or possibly some sort of group hysteria. *Words?* How could words kill?

Sasha loved to sing. Like any tween, ne spoke endlessly on nir phone with riends. Lately, I'd noticed the sudden frequent dropping of F-bombs in those conversations. Thinking about it now, it would have been impossible not to; ne meant for us to hear nir new, taboo lexicon.

It was obnoxious — the sort behavior that manifests when the hippest thing a child can come up with is being unnecessarily rude. I leaned around the corner and gave a disapproving look, which ne answered with an expression I can only interpret as saying, *Fuck off*.

Then, as Anna was preparing dinner one evening, I noticed her beauty, present even with her curls tied back and a sheen of steam and sweat glossing her face. I came near, hugging her from behind. My lovely Anna clamped my hands and shoved them away.

I'm cooking, she said. But her tone was clear. I was losing her. As nearly as I could tell, the only reason she did not either leave or kick me out was for Sasha's benefit.

In sprang our child. *Hey-hey*, I cheered. *How's Papa's little favorite?*

Sasha's retaliation was swift. With an expression of blazing contempt, nir eyes burned into mine. I yielded. I looked away. I was no good at this with nir at all, anymore, and nir talent for staring so fiercely that I backed down had manifested suddenly, out of nowhere.

An uncomfortable realization began to set in. In school, ne learned mathematical processes that I — and, indeed, most people my age — could no longer recall. Ne was learning things that those of my generation had already forgotten and had no day-to-day use for, and ne was being tested on nir grasp of them, all while being denied society's permission to even operate a simple motor vehicle. These realizations led nir to regard nirself as more intelligent than me, and more so than the vast majority of adults she met. Nir contempt for nir circumstances swelled.

Had my Papa's child disappeared completely into this scathing, caustic tween?

Anna bent down, away from the considerable white-noise racket of her stir-fry, went eye-to-eye with Sasha. Anaise beamed at nir mother.

What do you hear? Anna asked nir. It was simple, a vocabulary game we played. Sasha grinned, their faces not 10 inches apart.

Sizzle! Ne belted the word out at the top of nir lungs.

That word, *Sizzle* — so sibilant, all hissing and edges. A word like a blade, it sliced through Anna's beauty like a shattering windshield. It was the first manifestation, not yet at its full force, and I think that that is why Anna survived, though Sasha's word took a heavy toll: That sibilance slashed at Anna, a hurricane of razor blades, gashing open wounds and, ultimately, leaving her wheelchair-bound.

Where Anna's blood spilled, the kitchen transformed: Before I could even begin to wipe up the blood, the puddle, a deep cerise in color, began to grow. At first a handful of separate pools formed. Then those pools reached out to one another, slowly widening.Since that day it has slowly grown wider. I have tried lowering things in search of its bottom, but we can come by nothing as easily as before all of this, and when I upended a broom and dipped its handle in, I could not reach the bottom, and the slipped from my grasp and sank. The pool ranges from cobalt to robin's-egg blue, and shimmers subtlely, a vivid palette that contrasts with ours. The palette of our world seems to have drained to colorless shades of gray. I can see nothing through the surface of the pool. A freshwater scent wafts now from the room.

I cautiously navigate its edges to prepare what food I can forage from the abandoned stores. The laws that hold world together have come unmoored.

Before.2

No one knows what this is. It began around the time that the Voyager 1 spacecraft crossed the heliopause and left our solar system behind. Some saw connections in the timing. Parents around the world struggled to cope and adapt as their children's voices, without warning, suddenly became weaponized.

Some succumbed to religious speculations. Some new, or perhaps renewed, Curse of Babel. The gaunt, haunted, grubby man at the corner marked its coming by trading his large, homemade sign's slogan from "The End Is Nigh!" to:

"No More Launches!

G-D **Don't** Want Us

Up There In

HAEVIN!"

Perhaps, they postulated, in crossing the heliosphere, humankind had gone too far for His liking. Perhaps this was punishment He was visiting upon us. He had a reputation for that sort of thing. They struck out in desperate supposition, laboring to make sense of the vile new normal that pitted parents' survival against their children's most meager utterances.

After Anna's injury, I had to keep Sasha hidden. It quickly became clear that the streets were no longer safe for children. Roving packs of vigilantes, people who had avoided having offspring and who now felt besieged by them, would gun down a child on-sight, rather than risk being destroyed by a stray syllable. Often, the words felled them before they could get off a single shot.

Adults were never afflicted, never found that their speech had suddenly turned deadly. Not as far as we know, anyway. The change arrived so suddenly and with such devastating effect that civilization imploded. No communications, no television, no water or electricity. Children accidentally slaughtered their parents, teachers, any adults who were in the wrong place at the wrong time. Babies' nonsensical chatter chipped away at parents' defenses, driving them out of their minds or into retreat. The body count is unknowable, but it has been devastating.

Now.3

Anna abides, though with no spark, no enthusiasm for life, her former beauty now an intricate cicatrix and her flesh a papery, ashen gray. I do my best to balance helping her onto the toilet, wiping away the shit afterward, and keeping us fed. Outside, the world rages with the savagery that comes when such panic takes hold of a population that society shatters.

Looters have taken nearly all of the food from the Kwik-E Mart, the nearest convenience store. I find a couple of cans of creamed corn. Before all this I wouldn't have touched this stuff, but today, as I load them into my pack, the thought of it makes my stomach growl.

All of the stuff that's perishable rotted long ago, and other looters have taken most of the food that never rots.

Back at home, I put another log in the fireplace and move Anna closer for the warmth, but she sits, unresponsive. I hear no sound coming from Sasha's room, but to be as sure as I can, I wait a solid hour, listening, before I dare enter and replace nir gag. The arrangement isn't ideal. I do not dare let nir speak, lest nir words make short work of us. I keep nir hands and feet secured to a chair. I leave enough length on the ropes that ne can feed nirself, but not so much that ne can reach nir gag. We can barely communicate. I left a book on sign language on the table before nir months ago, but tied down as ne is, imprisoned by nir own father, ne sits, vacant-eyed and crestfallen. This time ne hasn't eaten a bite of the food I left with nir. I lock nir gag back in place.

In the kitchen, the pool in the floor's center has grown to a width of about five feet, a reflective, shimmering azure mirror. I can still make my way around it, but that won't be the case if it keeps widening. If our house had a basement, I would be able to examine it in more detail. But the place is built on swampy Florida land; the house stands on a concrete slab. The source of the pool, apart from its sanguinary beginning, is a mystery.

I struggle to open the cans of creamed corn with our dull, rusting can opener, then empty both cans into a saucepan. This I rest on our grill in the fireplace. It's not much, but it's food.

When I bring a hot bowl of the corn to Sasha, I see tears flowing from eyes blazing with fury.

If I un-gag you now, I whisper, *you'll say something so loud and so sibilant it will shred the flesh from my bones.*

But the rage in nir expression does not waver. Ne takes the pen in nir hand, hovers it over the notepad for a moment, then slashes out the word: *MONSTER.*

Fine, I tell nir. *You can eat it cold, later, when you're in a mood I can trust.*

I rejoin Anna before the fire. A questioning expression forms on heruined face.

Tough love, I'm afraid, I say. But my wife turns away. She hasn't a word for me — not a one.

Flow.1

The next morning, it is time to forage again. Our nearest neighbor was a professor emeritus of English, an immense man with thinning, wavy white hair who used to have dinner at our neighborhood pub every night. He has introduced himself to me a dozen times, with no recollection of the previous exchanges. I've been watching his house and, not having seen any activity there in more than a week, am contemplating pillaging there for whatever supplies he might have laid in.

Our days seem broken. I use terms such as *day* and *night*, but it is as though the planet has stopped its rotation; all day and all night, the sky and the air are an overcast, sullen gray.

I traverse the yard, entering the no-man's land between ours and his. This I do with care, because this retiree may, in fact, still remain within his home, and he may well be armed, and he'll certainly not find me familiar. The retiree's name is Morrow.

As I approach his home, I see and hear no signs of life. In fact, as I move nearer, I can see that one of his windows has shattered and gone unrepaired. I risk a glance into the place, but find no trace of Morrow. All is quiet inside, and the fireplace, though it was lit at some point in the past, shows signs that it burnt out long ago, and it has gone untended.

I find the front door closed, but unlocked. Inside, after a slow, wary reconnaissance, I decide that the old man must have fled. I find a few canned goods in his kitchen and load them into a bag — canned vegetables, a few soups, nothing much, though I cannot help but notice that Morrow's book shelves overflow with Atlases of rivers, streams, brooks, all manner of waterway. And it is a globe-spanning collection. As I try a final door, I am surprised to find stairs leading down: a basement! How unusual here, with our soggy soil. I brandish a fireplace lighter for what little light it can provide, and make my way down. The basement is musty and damp, with a plain concrete floor. Against the far wall, I spot sets of shelves that turn out to be Morrow's emergency supplies — a flashlight, a camping lantern, a gallon jug of water, and enough food to last us a few days. As I load what I can into my bag, the shelf I'm emptying wobbles a bit. I notice that the shelves each have a set of wheels attached at the bottom. In fact, now that I'm looking down here, near the floor, I see a set of arcs in the dust on the floor, growing out from beneath the shelves. I take hold of the shelf before me and, with an effort, roll it aside.

I find myself staring into the darkness of what is clearly some sort of tunnel. Its sides, ceiling, and floor all resemble the unfinished rock- and concrete-face of an abandoned sewage system, though these are clearly meant for human passage. Closer inspection with my meager flame reveals walls a claustrophobic four feet apart, along with a low, rough ceiling.

Over the next while, I explore the tunnel and find it labyrinthine. Why, I puzzle, would daft old Morrow's unlikely basement have a hidden door leading into a labyrinth? I spot a faint sapphire glow ahead of me, a blue light of some sort, and I decided to investigate. Reaching it means a long, uncertain walk.

Abruptly, the cramped tunnel opens into a yawning chamber, an aqua brilliance radiating from overhead. The ceiling appears to be ice, but as I watch, I notice that its surface is ungulating, stirred by some force. Somehow, I am standing submerged in a pond, its surface a ceiling moving slowly, more like cold molasses than water. A passage branches away from it to my right, another to my left. The one on my left seems to be flowing into the pond, and the snail-paced current of the one to the right flows away. I can feel the current's gentle pull. The floor of the passage is strewn with pebbles and silt, some of which glitter in the cobalt glow. Tiny debris drifts unhurriedly past, sparkling like tiny chunks of diamonds and ice.

Peering up through the shifting surface, I can make out the distorted façade of playground equipment, long fallen into disrepair, rusted and crumbling like everything else. The labyrinth — it is, somehow, a route decided by the flow of water through bodies and tributaries, ponds and creeks. That is enough for me to dub it the Flow, for shorthand.

I extinguish and pack my fireplace lighter. The Flow provides plenty of light. This space, somehow, seems to join the collective ebbs and tides, the current, the very flow of the waterways. And yet, I am walking normally, my feet on a floor of a million glimmering particles. I find things along the floor that seem out-of-place: A corroded piece of a ship bearing the identification "USS OKLAHOMA"; a mug and saucer, heavily encrusted with barnacles and shells, with "RMS Titanic" etched upon each; and shells, nacreous, phosphorous wonders from fresh- and saltwater creatures alike — all saturated in such color that they cast the washed-out world outside the Flow in a flat spectrum indeed.

I follow the passage whose current leads away, and after walking for more than an hour, my creek-passage opens into what has to be the river that runs alongside our town. I follow the stream's path, retracing my steps, and decide to investigate a branch I'd passed along my way out. The water of the aqua ceiling, here, does not seem to be in as much motion. I approach another pond-chamber. The floor of this one is much the same as the others, though a familiar broom rests in the silt at the bottom of this one. And, peering up through a small pool, I slowly come to recognize a room. I am staring up, through the watery ceiling, and into the kitchen of my own home.

Suddenly, Morrow's collection of waterway atlases makes a strange sort of sense to me. To follow the Flow, and to know where he was going, those maps would be useful.

Through the luminous ceiling I see cans and containers left open on the counter, and realize that Anna is the only one at home who could have gotten into the kitchen to get something to eat.

My heart soars: My wife will swoon with the news of my discovery, at all of its chromaticity and luminescence and wonder! I collect stones and shells, all glowing like gems. I will win her back. I begin stacking the stones, arranging them into geometrical patterns, making certain each placement is just so. I build a bower for my beloved — a wonder constructed of iridescent stones and glowing nacre. I can hardly wait to share my discovery of the labyrinth with her; so little new and exciting happens in our gray, cloistered world. I want to impress her, perhaps even delight her into some small conversation with my impossible find.

Then I realize that the discovery of this aquamarine labyrinth has immersed me in my curiosity so firmly that I've lost track of time. I've been stupid. I let the time get away from me. I have a seriously injured wife to care for and a reproachful, intemperate, and probably very hungry child to clean and feed. This transmarine ceiling is far too high for me to reach up and through. I hurriedly retrace my path to Morrow's basement and swing the shelving back into place.

I heave open the door to our home, brimming with excitement.

Anna! I call out, dropping my bag of filched foodstuffs in the entryway. No response comes.

Anna?

How long have I been gone? A terrifying notion strikes: What if the food I'd seen on our kitchen counter wasn't for Anna? What if I've been gone long enough that Anna felt it necessary to attempt to feed our child? The last time I'd laid eyes upon Sasha, the child had been in a vicious mood.

In a panic, I scramble down the hall toward Sasha's room. A chill wind pushes back my hair. When I reach nir room, the door is open. The scene on the other side is one of explosive, glistening scarlet and dull gray light from outside. The wall has been blown away.

Anna died here, shredded by our child's deadly lexicon.

There, sitting on the bed ne no longer uses, sits Sasha, weeping silently.

I weigh the risk to myself, then search out the notepad and pen.

Sasha, I write, *what happened?*

Sasha, with a trembling hand, takes the pen and pad.

Mama told me she loved me, ne writes.

In this bizarre moment, I cannot process Anna's demise; it does not seem either real or possible. I take back the pen and pad and write, *What then?*

Clearly reluctant to respond, my child regards the pad warily. After a long wait, ne reaches for the pen and pad. Ne protects me by allowing nirself neither to vocalize nir weeping nor to speak.

She brought me some food, ne writes. *She took off the gag and untied me. Then she told me she loves me. I started to sign "I love you," but then she told me it was ok* — she hesitates — *to say it out loud.*

Already, the room has begun to take on a cerulean glimmer. I suspect an actual blueshift may be beginning — that time may behave differently within the flow of the waterways and the areas immediately surrounding them.

We sit silently together as I turn the hand-cranked generator on our emergency radio and strain to hear a signal. Sasha has voluntarily blocked nir urge to speak by cutting cardboard down into a shape ne can squeeze between nir teeth and lips — a trick ne learned from a schoolmate who suffered Tourette Syndrome.

There's hardly ever anything to hear, but once in a while we catch a stray broadcast from someone with an emergency generator and a shortwave radio. The information that arrives is sometimes too outlandish to be believed. A survivalist hunkered down in the Hill Country outside Austin sometimes signs on. He calls himself the Minuteman. He is convinced that this is a zombie apocalypse. He does not leave his bunker. Every transmission from him sounds little more disconnected from the outside world than the previous one.

But his paranoia saved his life; laying in canned supplies, drinkable water, an emergency generator, and who knew what else, gave him and his wife a safe place to retreat to when the world as we knew it came crashing down.

I roll along the dial, searching ...

With my worn atlas, I open to the maps of Florida. I could find a path to Cape Canaveral easily enough, but the open road? That's just asking for trouble. But Morrow's trove of waterway atlases?

I'm going to forage, I tell my child. Ne sits in a chair near the window, reading by the colorless light from outside. Ne does not look up.

I return to Morrow's basement. I haven't told Sasha about the transmarine labyrinth yet. I don't know whether ne'll believe me when I do. But I want to see what more I can find among its watery branches. Above the fluid ceiling, I see what I can of the world. Everything moves in slow motion, as though it's all swimming in syrup. I follow the branch that leads to the pool in our kitchen, and happen across a new passage. Through the surface, I watch as Sasha's room comes into focus overhead. The blood spilled in Anna's death has created a reflecting pool like the one in my kitchen.

I am thinking, now, of the canned foods I'm going to look for, when the current strengthens, the Flow lifting me from the floor. I reach for the wall, but only scrape up my hand in the effort. Tendrils of my blood swirl into my wake. My pulse quickens. This hasn't happened in my earlier visits to the labyrinth, and I do not know where this rush of the Flow is heading.

Abruptly, the current ebbs and the water becomes — well — water again. It happens so suddenly that water rushes into my nose and throat. My clothes suddenly soaked and heavy, the Flow vomits me forth, and I land in the grass beside a storm-sewer ditch. The tiny trickle of man-made stream that runs through here could not possibly have been deep enough for me to submerge.

I've gulped so much water into my lungs that I spend the next few minutes vomiting it back up. When I've righted myself reasonably, I look to the shore. Just up from the ditch is a building that used to be a grocery. I plod a muddy trudge up and away from the sewer.

I negotiate my way around, checking for others. When I'm reasonably certain the coast is clear, I force open a locked rear door. The gut-wrenching stench of rotted meat and vegetables makes me wretch, but I have nothing left to expel.

I wring water from my bag, and it splatters to the floor. There are obviously no lights to turn on, so I make my way in what bland, flat daylight seeps in through the place's translucent ceiling. I find rows and rows of foodstuffs in cans and jars. The produce and meat sections of the store were clearly left to rot when the world broke and the power failed. I load my bag, planning to carry as much preserved food as possible out, then figure out how to get it home from wherever I am.

Back at home, as I roll the tuning dial, searching, I hear a faint voice — so faint that I almost don't catch it. I've been cranking the radio's manual power and listening long enough that I've let myself space off; I'd stopped paying attention.

The signal is faint, but after rolling back over the frequencies a few times, I find it again. It's another survivor. *The sky is radiant*, she reports. *To anyone who can hear me — and I don't know if anyone can — it is an eerie blue, sort of faint when I first noticed it, but I ventured out earlier today and witnessed the glow growing stronger. It seemed to be flowing toward a specific, single location. I had pepper spray, in case I found any trouble, but the streets here in Cape Canaveral were dead. This place is a ghost town.*

The brightest concentration of the glow was almost neon. It converges from all directions at the bottom of Launch Platform 41, then shoots up and away, a line of light going straight up.

Canaveral LC-41?, I say. Sasha raises nir eyebrows, forming a curious expression. Ne lifts nir hands and shrugs nir shoulders. It's faster than writing or signing.

Voyager 1 launched from LC-41, I tell her.

Ne rolls nir eyes at me and slashes out a message with nir pen and pad: *WHY THE FUCK DOES THAT MATTER?!?*

I feel foolish. Stupid. She has me. I don't know.

The voice from the shortwave continues. *Time is behaving oddly at the platform. The closer I got, the more things around me slowed down. I watched a bird hang standstill in midflight about a block ahead of me. I think it might stop altogether at the LC. It might even flow backwards.*

The signal fades.

Cape Canaveral, I say. I can feel its pull, a current flowing toward LC-41.

Sasha regards me warily. We've settled into a necessarily tacit truce, but nir showing any sign of being impressed by me or my actions is rare. I can't blame nir. If I were a dependent child and my lone surviving parent showed signs that he was losing his mind, I'd be worried.

But the Flow — why is it flowing toward the LC?

I think we need to go on a roadtrip, I tell Sasha.

Ne raises nir eyebrows dubiously at me. I open one of Morrow's atlases to a map showing Cape Canaveral.

Come on, I say, *I have something to show you. Something I've found.*

I lead my silent child across the way to Morrow's house, then through the door and down to the basement.

Stand back, I tell nir, and ne listens. I swing the shelving aside, unveiling the labyrinth and the bower I built to lure Anna.

I call it the Flow, I tell nir. *Come on.* I hold out my hand and, thankfully, ne takes it.

I don't quite know how, but the flow seems to unite every river, stream, creek, whatever sort of waterway — the circulatory system of the planet — even blood, as it travels the labyrinth of the body. And the flow of time.

Now Sasha wears an expression of fear. I try to soothe nir, keeping my voice calm, authoritative. *I don't know what happened, but that woman on the shortwave? What she reported has me thinking that the old launchpads at Cape Canaveral are important, somehow. Come on. I'll show you.*

I lead my child along the passage and into the first chamber of the Flow.

I hug nir, pull nir close; ne stiffens a bit, but relaxes after a few seconds.

Hold on.

I hold the map of Cape Canaveral before me and concentrate on its location.

A moment later, the Flow's current gathers us up from the floor and hurtles us along a vortex of the liquid that we can, inexplicably, breathe.

When the flow ejects us in a crashing wave, we find ourselves gasping, spitting water, just outside the Launch Complex. Sasha tugs excitedly at my shirt sleeve, and points up.

The sky overhead, the ground beneath us, everything radiates a neon blue hue, all of it flowing toward the one I recognize as LC-41. There, the Flow gathers at the base of the platform, turning upward in a bolt of brilliance, into the sky. And I know what is at the other end of that beam of light: It's Voyager 1, stationary out there, somewhere, anchored by the Flow to our broken world. Voyager, the flow of time, the impossible physics that made the children's words lethal, all of it is part of the Flow, somehow.

Without thinking about it, I close a hand around my locket. *But if time is behaving strangely at the LC —* I say. *Come on.*

I lift my child to nir feet and we set off for the center of the Flow: LC-41.

At the base of the Launch Complex, I can see everything slowing more and more, the closer we come. Sasha pulls on my sleeve again, shaking nir head.

I need to try something, I tell nir. Ne swallows, then nods uncertainly.

We approach a bird, stationary in flight in the air before us, shining like a jeweled sculpture in brilliant sunshine.

I fumble for my locket and open it, extracting the lock of Anna's hair. This I plunge forward, ahead of the bird, to where the effect might be even stronger. And with a quiver, the lock of hair begins to lengthen. Sasha shakes my sleeve, pointing at the hair. It's growing.

I know, I say.

And as we watch, the hair grows. The gray begins to disappear from it. And it begins to take on the shape of a woman, the radiant cobalt glow becoming blinding.

Noah? she says.

In the heart of the glow stands Anna, younger than she was when Sasha's loving, deadly words struck nir down. Younger, in fact, than she had been when she began to become distant toward me.

It's me, I tell her. *It's us.*

I release the lock and place a hand on my wife's shoulder, leading nher out, toward us.

Sasha weeps, but here, in the heart of the Flow, the sound does not transform into an attack on the flesh. *Mama!* she says, *I am so, so sorry.*

For what? Anna asks.

Nevermind, I say. She does not remember the events leading to nir death, nor, apparently, the distance that had grown between us before the world as we knew it collapsed. I place a hand on Sasha's shoulder now, and we shared a long, heartfelt hug.

In the distance, I see a young man, immobile mid-leap, one who is somehow familiar. After some time, if there is such a thing in this place, I recognize Morrow, returned to youth and health, stationary in the Flow.

I don't know how this works, I tell them. *Present and past seem to have collapsed into this moment. We might not be able to leave the Flow. We might have to stay right here, at the heart of the Flow and the fracture, where Anna can be gone, yet alive, and Sasha can be both male and female, or neither.*

Minnows

"Minnows," first appeared in Writing that Risks: New Work from Beyond the Mainstream, Red Bridge Press, July 2013, and was nominated for a Pushcart Award

fishie 1.1 "Fed your fish yet?" our mother asks. I say I will. Blue follows after me like a stink I can't scrub off. I pick up the little container full of flakes and Blue says, "How much do we give 'em?"

"A pinch," I say.

"How much is that?"

"What? It's a pinch."

"A big pinch or a little pinch?'

"Jeez, Blue, I don't know."

Blue is quiet for a few seconds, so I pinch a pinch of fish food and throw it on the top of the water.

"What's fish food taste like?" he asks.

2.1 We're family, and families solve their own problems.

0.11 Our mother is awake, but her eyes are dark all around and the skin there wrinkles dry in a web of wrinkles. I tell her I'll make mac and cheese for dinner later and she tells us to sit down.

minnows 1.1 Pop-Pop comes home from work with two smallish goldfish in a baggie full of cloudy water. "Pets for my boys!" he yells, "My little men! You two get to name 'em." Pop-Pop goes to the back porch and fishes out a glass tank I always knew was there but didn't know was for fish. He takes it out the back door and hoses it out out back, then brings it back in and sets it on the little table in the dining room. He gives my brother and me each a pan and says, "Fill 'er up!"

5.1 Later, I make our last box of mac and cheese and some powdered milk. There's still a little powdered milk left after. July is burning out from under us and our Pop-Pop is gone and I can't make our mother listen. I leave a bowl of mac and cheese outside her door, but know that in the morning it will be un-ate.

In the morning, the bowl of mac and cheese is right where I left it. Our mother hasn't touched it and she still isn't getting out of bed.

1.1a *In the night, I dream of Pop-Pop attacking the house, smashing in all of the ground-floor windows and yelling our mother's name.*

4.1 In the morning I wake up to someone knocking on the front door. **Outside is my Uncle Jim. He smiles and says "Mornin'. Your Pop-Pop here?"**
"No," I tell him. "My mother says he might not come back."
"Where's your phone?"
"We don't have to tell anyone," I say.

3.1 In the morning I wake up to someone knocking on the front door. Outside, Gwen-Doe-Lyne and a cop car have pulled up.
Our mother is shaking.
"What'd you do to our mother?" I say.
She says, "I didn't do nothing. Your pop happened to her."
Our mother is silent and shaking. The cop is actually helping her up the front steps.

2.2 We're family, and families solve their own problems. **We police our own. It's no one else's business**.

0.10 Our mother is awake, but her eyes are dark all around and the skin there wrinkles dry in a web of wrinkles. I tell her I'll make mac and cheese for dinner later and she tells us to sit down. **"Your Pop-Pop isn't probably coming back," she tells us.**
    I say, "What?"
    "Your Pop-Pop," she says, and she shakes when she breathes, "isn't probably coming back."

minnows 1.2 ~~Pop-Pop comes home from work with two smallish goldfish in a baggie full of cloudy water.~~ "Pets for my boys!" he yells~~, "My little men! You two get to name 'em." Pop-Pop goes to the back porch and fishes out a glass tank I always knew was there but didn't know was for fish. He takes it out the back door and hoses it out out back, then brings it back in and sets it on the little table in the dining room. He gives my brother and me each a pan and~~ says, "Fill 'er up!"

We do. Pop-Pop puts some drops in the tank and we float the baggie in there a while, then let out the fish. "Goldfish?" I say. "Dime feeders," he says to me.

Interstitial 1.1　It's even hotter today, and getting worse and the air heavier. Hotter and hotter, it's getting late in June and our mother and Pop-Pop fight harder and drink harder against the heat. They go to bed yelling and wake up in sweat.

Our mother tries to run a good house, keep a good home, she tells us that and she makes us dust and do dishes and pick up to show us how it's done right. Dinner, our mother always tells us, is a sit-down meal at the table at 5:30 sharp. Last time I stayed out of sight behind her garden and pretended I didn't hear her calling, she put me in bed — *hungry*! — at seven o'clock! I just laid there, bored and hungry.

A Friday and hotter and

1.1b *In the night, I dream of Pop-Pop attacking the house, smashing in all of the ground-floor windows and yelling our mother's name.* **Gwen-Doe-Lyne is Our Mother's friend. She's still around, and that seems to make him angrier,** *'cause she's an outsider. She don't understand.*

0.9　Our mother is awake, but her eyes are dark all around and the skin there wrinkles dry in a web of wrinkles. ~~I tell her I'll make mac and cheese for dinner later and she tells us to sit down.~~ "Your Pop-Pop isn't probably coming back," she tells us. **I don't know what I hear, but that's what she sounded like she said.** I say, "What?"

"Your Pop-Pop," she says, and she shakes when she breathes, "isn't probably coming back."

Blue sobs next to me.

minnows 2.1　My brother and me cross the empty field that's growing where it looks like a house should be there but it isn't, past the house that's haunted and its broke-out windows, and grab super-sour gooseberries from the gooseberry bush on our dirt path. The dirt path goes back into the woods here, and down at the end of it is the sewer grate and the big concrete pipe that pours into it. It's warm enough I'm sure I'm getting more pets today. The minnows will be swimming around in the sewer-pond, where concrete spills onto rocks and mud. Minnows maybe. Frogs even, maybe.

the musty-wet air all over us, and our mother is in the kitchen making pork cutlets and hamburger helper and cut canned corn. She runs a good house and she keeps a good home. And dinner is at 5:30. And when it's 102 degrees out and the blacktop melts between your toes until your feet are too hot to stay standing on it, and the hot comes up in waves that make the air move like water, and Pop-Pop hasn't made it home by 5:15 to get cleaned up for a sit-down meal at the table, her anger hangs in the air, thick with sweat. And at 5:20, the whole house has got hotter, like it's gonna blow apart. And at 5:45, when Pop-Pop pulls in the old white car, she's just waiting. She served the rest of us at 5:30, but she's just waiting.

In the tank, the goldfish chase and the water is getting hazy. Pop-Pop is a smog of Pabst Blue Ribbon and cigarettes and our mother's patience with him ran out long before he got his last ones for the road.

"Dinner at 5:30 means dinner at 5:30 in this house!" she shrieks. My ears ring. Blue starts to put

The woods are thicker here than back in the neighborhood, by the houses. But the pond is our secret. We can be pirates here, or Indians. We like pirates more, so we named it Pirate's Cove. I catch tadpoles and put pond water in my jar for them, then close the lid tight.

1.1c *In the night, I dream of Pop-Pop attacking the house, smashing in all of the ground-floor windows and yelling our mother's name. Gwen-Doe-Lyne is Our Mother's friend. She's still around, and that seems to make him angrier, 'cause she's an outsider. She don't understand.*
Our mother tries to leave us. She's's stuck as we are. I wake to Gwen-Doe-Lyne and my mother smoking in the kitchen. "Careful there junior," she says, "Lotta glass broke here last night."

5.2 ~~Later,~~ I make our last box of mac and cheese and some powdered milk. ~~There's still a little powdered milk left after. July is burning out from under us and o~~ Our Pop-Pop is gone and I can't make our mother listen. I leave a bowl of mac and cheese outside her door, but know that in the morning it will be un-ate.

In the morning, the bowl of mac and cheese is right where I left it. Our mother hasn't touched it and she still isn't getting out of bed, **and our Pop-Pop still isn't around**.

4.2 ~~In the morning I wake up to someone knocking on the front door. Outside is m~~My Uncle Jim. ~~He~~ smiles and says "Mornin'. Your Pop-Pop here?"

"No," I tell him. "My mother says he might not come back."

his fingers in his ears, but I shake my head and make an *I'm serious* face and he stops.

And Pop-Pop is pleading with her, telling her he's sorry, he had car trouble, and she says bullshit, I smell the bar on you, and I have to admit she's right, already I noticed that, but I'm not no way gonna say it. And it explodes. They explode. They yell and she throws hot food and a skillet at him and Blue and I know we can't be around in the middle of one of these and we run for it.

Uncle Jim looks afraid, real afraid for a second, then wipes it off his face. "Where's she?" I point into the house.

Inside, the dishes have piled high and crusty and stuff is all over the carpets and floors.

"My God," says Uncle Jim. "Have you been eating?"

"Yeah!" I say. "I'm the man of the house now. I've been cooking."

Jim looks around at the dishes and the mess. "You're the man?"

"Yeah," I say, "Pop-Pop told me so before he left. It's family business, no one else's. We don't have to tell anyone. Especially not those pigs."

"Where's your phone?"

"We don't have to tell anyone," I say.

"Show me."

1.2 *In the night, I dream of Pop-Pop attacking the house, smashing in all of the ground-floor windows and yelling our mother's name. Gwen-Doe-Lyne is Our Mother's friend.* ~~She's still around~~, *and that seems to make him angrier,* ~~'cause she's an outsider. She don't understand.~~

Our mother tries to leave us. ~~Our mother, though, will not leave us, not while that lid is held down tight.~~ She's's stuck as we are. ~~I wake to~~ Gwen-Doe-Lyne ~~and my mother smoking in the kitchen.~~ ~~"Careful there junior,"~~ she says, "Lotta glass broke here last night."

"Where's Pop-Pop?" I say.

"Where he belongs," says Gwen-Doe-Lyne. Our mother's eyes are unfocussed, reflecting.

0.8 Our mother is awake, but her eyes are dark all around and the skin there wrinkles dry in a web of wrinkles. "Your Pop-Pop isn't probably coming back," she tells us.

~~I don't know what I hear, but that's what she sounded like she said.~~ I say, "What?"

"Your Pop-Pop," she says, and she shakes when she breathes, "isn't probably coming back."
Blue sobs next to me, **and then the words are just shooting out of me. "Let him come back," I say.**

minnows 2.2 When our mother sees us, her eyes are puffy even though it's lunch time. The hit
one isn't much more puffy than the not-hit one. But sitting there, in the kitchen, in rollers and a
cloud of smoke from her smokes, she looks tired. Then her eyes find us through the clouds, and
they get wide.
I hold up my jar and holler, "Tadpoles!" The tadpoles make me so happy I know they'll have to
make her happy too. In the tank, one fish runs, the other chases.
Our mother pinches the cigarette between two fingers and points to the back porch. "Not in my
house," she says, shaking her big, roller-lumpy head. "I keep a good home." She grinds out the
butt, that's what my Pop-Pop calls it, her butt, in the too-full ashtray. She sneezes and ash
swirls in the air, real slow, the sun through it like a giant sword.
I turn for the porch, but the jar slips and smashes on the floor, dumping sewer-pond water and
breaking glass and flapping tadpoles in a big, slow crash.

3.2 In the morning I wake up to someone knocking on the front door. Outside, Gwen-Doe-Lyne
and a cop car have pulled up.
Our mother is **silent and** shaking. **She has long scratches on her hands and her feet and
her arms and her legs with black string like bugs' legs sticking out down both sides.
Stitches. I've had stitches.**
~~"What'd you do to our mother?" I say.~~
~~She says, "I didn't do nothing. Your pop happened to her."~~
The cop is actually helping her up the front steps.

0.8a "I want him back. I want things back the way they were."
2.3 We're family, and families solve their own problems. **None of the other kids talk about
their pops hitting their moms — that's not how we do it.** We police our own, no cops, Pop-
Pop said to us. Even Uncle Jim beats up Pop-Pop in private. It's no one else's business.

4.3 My Uncle Jim smiles and says

"Have you been eating?"

"I'm the man of the house now. I've been cooking."

"You're the man?"

"Yeah," I say, "Pop-Pop told me so before he left. It's family business, no one else's. We don't have to tell anyone. Especially not those pigs." **Uncle Jim jumps a bit at my words. He knocks on our mother's door, says her name. Then he comes back to me.**

"Where's your phone?"

"We don't have to tell anyone," I say.

"Show me."

I lead him into the kitchen and show him the phone on the wall. He picks it up, then gives it a funny look and hits the button a few times. Then he puts it back, shaking his head.

"Do you have any friends who live close?" he says.

0.7 Our mother is awake, but her eyes are dark all around and the skin there wrinkles dry in a web of wrinkles. "Your Pop-Pop isn't probably coming back," she tells us.

I say, "What?"

"Your Pop-Pop," she says, and she shakes when she breathes, "isn't probably coming back."

~~Blue sobs next to me, and then t~~ The words are just shooting out of me. "Let him come back," I say. **She says, "I don't want to."**

minnows 2.3 ~~When e~~ Our mother sees us~~, her eyes are puffy even though it's lunch time. The hit one isn't much more puffy than the not-hit one. But sitting there, in the kitchen, in rollers and a cloud of smoke from her smokes, she looks tired. Then her eyes find us through the clouds, and they get wide~~.

"How the hell did you boys get so filthy? It's not even lunchtime!" she says. I look down at my shirt and see the dirt and mud. Blue is worse, though, he's got mud in his ears somehow.

I turn for the porch, but the jar slips and smashes on the floor, dumping sewer-pond water and breaking glass and flapping tadpoles in a big, slow crash. Our mother hits the roof, screaming at us to look at the mess we made and clean up the mess we made. Blue bolts out the front door and I scramble out the screen window with no screen in it, onto the thing that's supposed to hold up an air conditioner, and away. I sneak a big canning jar from Pop-Pop's rusty lawnmower shed. I catch more tadpoles at Pirate's Cove and chase minnows. Blue finds me there after a while, tells me he wants to go home. "Not yet," I say. "Let her cool off. You see how she goes after Pop-Pop. We'll go later."

0.7a "~~I want him back.~~ I want things back way they were!"
".were they way the back things want I"

0.6 ~~Our mother is awake, but her eyes are dark all around and the skin there wrinkles dry in a web of wrinkles. "Your Pop-Pop isn't probably coming back," she tells us.~~
~~I say, "What?"~~
~~"Your Pop-Pop," she says, and she shakes when she breathes, "isn't probably coming back."~~
The words are just shooting out of me. "Let him come back," I say. She says, "I don't want to."
This is insane. We're a family.
I make each word weigh the same. "Let. Him. Come. Back."
"I don't want to," she says, and her voice is sad, so sad.
"Why are you so sad? All you have to do is let him come back," I say.
Later, I make our last box of mac and cheese and some powdered milk. There's still a little powdered milk left after. July is burning out from under us and our Pop-Pop is gone and I can't make our mother listen. I leave a bowl of mac and cheese outside her door, but know that in the morning it will be un-ate.

1.3 *In the night, ~~I dream of Pop-Pop attacking the house, smashing in all of the ground-floor windows and yelling our mother's name. Gwen-Doe-Lyne is Our Mother's friend. She's still around, and that seems to make him angrier, 'cause she's an outsider. She don't understand.~~ the four of us are on a beach at Lake Okoboji. We're swimming in Lake Okoboji, water that's clear like glass. The rocks on the bottom are exactly the shape and size of turtles, and I can barely pick one up to swim with it to the top to prove to everyone it's a turtle, and when I get there, it has turned into a rock to fool me. I try and try, but the turtles keep turning into rocks until finally my Pop-Pop, shaking his head, tells me to knock it off. Then we're all four, our mother, Blue, me, and my Pop-Pop in the lead, swimming, but the water is dirtier than Okoboji, because it's Pirate's Cove, and we're minnows, and gigantic people appear right over top of us and try to catch us. Pop-Pop and our mother chase all wild, one thumping into the other, both hurting both, till one, Pop-Pop leaves through the roof of the pond and swims up, out, and away. In the commotion the water has gotten swirled up and hard to see through, but a big blade of sun cuts down through the swirl. My lungs burn and a net scrapes across my face and body and sploosh, I'm in a fish tank. With a thunk, a rock the size and shape of a turtle lands on the lid — a rock bigger than any of us.*

Our mother tries to leave us. **Our mother, though, will not leave us, not while that lid is held down tight. She's's stuck as we are.** ~~Gwen-Doe-Lyne says, "Lotta glass broke here last night."~~ ~~"Where's Pop-Pop?" I say.~~

~~"Where he belongs," says Gwen-Doe-Lyne.~~ Our mother's eyes are unfocussed, reflecting. **Like a fish's.**

0.6a "I want things back way they were!"

„˙ǝɹǝʍ ʎǝɥʇ ʎɐʍ ʞɔɐq sƃuᴉɥʇ ʇuɐʍ I„

0.5 The words are just shooting out of me. "Let him come back," I say. She says, "I don't want to."

This is insane. We're a family.

I make each word weigh the same. "Let. Him. Come. Back."

"I don't want to," she says, and her voice is sad, so sad.

"Why are you so sad? All you have to do is let him come back," I say.

"It isn't that easy," she says. I look around, and I want it all to make sense and it doesn't. The fish tank is thick with algae and swirled-up stuff. Our Mother drifts, her eyes dull like a deep-sea fish's, one that doesn't use its eyes much. It still doesn't make sense.

"I'll make us mac and cheese," I say. In my head I can hear Pop-Pop, my Pop-Pop, telling Blue to listen to me, telling me to take care of our mother, telling me I'm the man of the house. "It'll be okay. I'm the man of the house." *Don't take too much shit from'er, but take care of'er*, he'd said.

minnows 2.4 We don't dare go back for lunch. I let Blue drop minnows he catches in my jar with my tadpoles. The tadpoles won't mind. It keeps him too busy to worry about going back yet.

When we get back, we go in through the back door and I put this jar on a shelf on the back porch real, real careful. Blue says to me something about fish needing air, and that's stupid, fish breathe water, so I tell him to shut up.

Our mother is in bed again, and Pop-Pop is still. In the kitchen I find Wonderbread and steak sauce and make us no-steak steak sandwiches. I mix an envelope of Kool-Aid in a plastic pitcher in the sink and stir with my hand in almost to the elbow to reach the bottom. The one goldfish hits the lid so hard it flips a little open, then claps back closed.

minnows 3.1 When our mother wakes for the afternoon she takes a long, long time showering. There's sticky red on the counter where I spilled pouring us Kool-Aid, and ashy mud near the ashtray. Our mother steps from her room, calls us gross little monsters, and orders us to the back yard. She hoses the mud off of us and says our clothes are done for. In the night, I hear the goldfish chasing, chasing, and once in a while, the thump of the one or the other one hitting the lid.

0.5a "I want things back way they were!"
  "I want things back way they were!"

0.4 ~~Our mother is awake, but her eyes are dark all around and the skin there wrinkles dry in a web of wrinkles. "Your Pop-Pop isn't probably coming back," she tells us.~~
~~I say, "What?"~~
~~"Your Pop-Pop," she says, and she shakes when she breathes, "isn't probably coming back."~~

Interstitial 1.2 In the woods along our path, Boy-O Sparks and the other older boys swing and jump through the trees, hooting like chimps. When he's around the older boys, Boy-O doesn't want much to do with us. We know to stay out later still when we see the red lights flashing from our place.

We catch lightning bugs and smear their glowing stuff on our faces for war paint, until the lightning bugs aren't out anymore and the glowing stuff doesn't glow anymore. We get back late to no one at home. Broken dishes and food exploded all over. I dig around in the kitchen and find us peanut butter and jelly and make us one-slice Wonderbread sandwiches and wild berry Kool-Aid. Blue seems real, real sad, but he gets a red Kool-Aid mustache, and when I show him in the mirror, he laughs. The phone rings but I don't pick it up. No one told me what we're supposed to tell

The words are just shooting out of me. "Let him come back," I say. She says, "I don't want to."

This is insane. We're a family.

I make each word weigh the same. "Let. Him. Come. Back."

"I don't want to," she says, and her voice is sad, so sad.

"Why are you so sad? All you have to do is let him come back," I say.

Later, I make our last box of mac and cheese and some powdered milk. There's still a little powdered milk left after. July is burning out from under us and our Pop-Pop is gone and I can't make our mother listen. I leave a bowl of mac and cheese outside her door, but know that in the morning it will be un-ate.

Everything zeroes here.

anyone who asks. And like Pop-Pop said, we're a family. We fix our own problems. They're no one else's business.

Blue and I got lots of bug bites outside tonight. I find the pink lotion our mother uses for those and paint them all pink.

minnows 3.2 In the morning, on the back porch, the tadpoles and the minnows float at the top of the closed-lidded jar. In the dining room the goldfish pester each other.

0.4a I make each word weigh the same. "Let. Him. Come. Back."

"I don't want to," she says, and her voice is sad, so sad.

"Why are you so sad? All you have to do is let him come back," I say.

"It isn't that easy," she says. I look around, and I want it all to make sense and it doesn't. The fish tank is thick with algae and swirled-up stuff. Our Mother drifts, her eyes dull like a deep-sea fish's, one that doesn't use its eyes much. It still doesn't make sense.

Everything zeroes here. in four ...

fishie 1.2 *What's fish food taste like?!* This I had not thought of asking. "It smells like Pirate's Cove mud," I say.

"Yeah, but what does it *taste* like?"

"It's good. Like catfish. Here, stick out your tongue."

Blue smiles and out comes his tongue. I smear it with a really, really big pinch, and Blue's smile disappears in a burst of barf that covers his chin, but doesn't go anywhere else. It won't be good if our mother sees it. I drag him into my brother's and me's bedroom and our bathroom and washcloth him off.

0.3 Our Mother drifts, her eyes dull like a deep-sea fish's~~, one that doesn't use its eyes much. It still doesn't make sense~~.
"I'll make us mac and cheese," I say. In my head I can hear Pop-Pop, my Pop-Pop, telling Blue to listen to me, telling me to take care of our mother, telling me I'm the man of the house. ~~"It'll be okay. I'm the man of the house."~~ *Don't take too much shit from'er~~, but take care of'er~~,* he'd said. Our mother says my name, Pop-Pop's name, and I explode, looking for weakness. ~~Everything zeroes here. in four~~ **three ...**

4.4 "We don't have to tell anyone," I say.
I lead him into the kitchen and show him the phone on the wall. He picks it up, then gives it a funny look and hits the button a few times. Then he puts it back, shaking his head.
"Do you have any friends who live close?" he says.
I nod. "Boy-O and his family the Sparkses are only a mile and a half or so down."
Uncle Jim thumbs through the phone book and writes out a number on our notepad and hands it to me. "I need you to go to Boy-O's house and tell his pop you have an emergency, and to get an ambulance here."

0.2 Our Mother drifts, her eyes dull like a deep-sea fish's
"I'll make us mac and cheese," I say. In my head I can hear Pop-Pop, my Pop-Pop, telling Blue to listen to me, telling me to take care of our mother, telling me I'm the man of the house. *Don't take too much shit from'er* he'd said.
Our mother says my name, Pop-Pop's name, and I explode, looking for weakness.
~~three~~ **two ...**

0.1 ~~Our mother says my name, Pop-Pop's name, and~~ I'm ~~explode,~~ looking for weakness **in her**. I point to her cuts from the flying glass.
"You let him come back or I'll hit you in the stitches!"
Our mother's mouth opens big and round for a second, then closes, and her eyes glaze over, dead like a carp's. Her mouth opens again, big and round, but I can't hear any air going in or out. She stands, wobbly, and drifts into her room, closing the door. Then we hear the click of the lock locking.

30

~~two~~ **one ...**

minnows 3.3 In the dining room the goldfish pester each other. **They're going crazy in that tank.**

0.0 I point to ~~her~~ **Our Mother's** cuts from the flying glass.
"You let him come back or I'll hit you in the stitches!"
 Our mother's mouth opens big and round for a second, then closes, and her eyes glaze over, dead like a carp's. Her mouth opens again, big and round, but I can't hear any air going in or out. She stands, wobbly, and drifts into her room, closing the door. Then we hear the click of the lock locking.

3.3 ~~In the morning I wake up to someone knocking on the front door. Outside, Gwen-Doe-Lyne and a cop car have pulled up.~~
~~The cop is actually helping her up the front steps.~~
"You the man of the house?" says the cop. He seems friendly. That's not right. I nod, wary.
"Your pop gave her quite a scare tonight," says the cop.
I nod. *We police our own,* **I think.**
"Know where he's keeping himself?" says the cop. I knew it. He wants us to break ranks, rat each other out. "Nope," I say, then realize it's true. Pop-Pop was never happy to see the cops visit. Why should I be any different?

4.5 ~~"We don't have to tell anyone," I say.~~
~~I lead him into the kitchen and show him the phone on the wall. He picks it up, then gives it a funny look and hits the button a few times. Then he puts it back, shaking his head.~~
~~"Do you have any friends who live close?" he says.~~
~~I nod. "Boy-O and his family the Sparkses are only a mile and a half or so down."~~
Uncle Jim thumbs through the phone book and writes out a number on our notepad and hands it to me. "I need you to go to Boy-O's house and tell his pop you have an emergency, and to get an ambulance here."
"Aye-aye, cap'n," I say and salute him. It's a game: I'll be a spy behind Nazi German lines on a mission.
He watches me for a second, then returns my salute.

"Go *now*," he says.

The Good Life

"The Good Life" first appeared in Phoebe – A Journal of Literature and Arts, Vol 36, Issue 1, Spring 2007.

We'd been laying low, trying to fly below the radar, dodging the landlord we owed nearly a year of back rent. We opted to live the good life, staying in a Days Inn with a pool. We guarded what little actual cash we had. I didn't have any money in the account, but I still had checks.

That year had gone by so fast, with me in and out of work and mostly out. I slept off a hangover, missing my first shift at a Burger King, and that made my eyes tear up. It was dark in the bedroom, that kind of lifeless gray you get when the light of a cloudy day reflects off the snow. We'd had a snowstorm overnight, and the house was fucking freezing.

"Jesus Christ," I said, feeling about as much self-worth as I thought the voluntarily homeless must, "I can't even keep a job at Burger King." I had $37 to my name and no paycheck on the horizon. It was winter, and in Iowa, they can't cut your utilities while it's still freezing out, so I could let that bill slide a while.

The whole thing pushed me to the edge; I was ready to lose it, promise to clean up and take the straight and narrow right there on the spot. But there she was to keep me from any hasty decisions. Lee Ann. The housemate who came to the dilapidated dive on Dodge and decided to stay. She'd just come walking up the walk one day late in the summer. Shitty, my bartender over at a place called the Fox Head, had hired her to wait tables. When she'd mentioned that she was looking for an apartment, he'd sent her my way. I didn't remember telling Shitty that I needed roommates, but I was perched at his bar a lot in those days, and didn't always recall absolutely everything I told him.

So anyway, right, Shitty sent her strolling down the cracked sidewalk out front of my place one painfully sunny late-summer morning as I sat with Larry. We were wincing our way through a Maxwell House, post-acid hangover. I was trying to read a week-old newspaper, but you know that post-acid funk, all greasy and skin-crawly, your insides feeling all squeezed. Your brain just doesn't work right. I was mostly just spacing off.

She grinned at us, told us her name. She took one look at the place and decided that the $100 rent was right for her. Larry seemed a little uncomfortable with the idea of a girl roommate even then, thinking back on it.

A prodigious flow of Old Style across the bar from Shitty that first night, and we closed out the bar for a two a.m. walk to the place we all three now called home. Though I suspect the beer had something to do with it, she decided that first night it was time to fuck me.

Like I said, that was late in the summer. I was a night janitor part time. I cleaned a building that belonged to Kirkwood College. During the day, people who wanted to stay in school after high school came to the small brick satellite on Maiden Lane; at night, loaded up on whatever I could afford, I came through and cleaned up after them. I emptied their garbage cans, bleached their toilets and urinals, swept and mopped their floors. I wondered if they ever thought about where the garbage and stains went. No one from the school was ever around when I showed up for work.

My boss, Danno, came by unannounced sometimes to show me where I'd missed a cobweb, things like that. Guess it made him feel smart, necessary, like no one but him could see a cobweb and have that light bulb come on in their head, telling them that it should come down. I didn't keep that job long. With a meager drinking budget from the job, I needed to cut back somewhere. Lee Ann and me decided to room together and sublet the extra. The idea was, that would drop the rent to $50 each, except that we never found anyone to take my old room, so it just stayed empty.

So, the Burger King morning, I was about to make some barrel-chested proclamation that enough was enough or something and go out and try to save my new job. I had a splitting hangover headache and bruises on my chest and shoulders where Lee Ann had punched me the night before in a fight over something. I don't remember what. But then, like a champ, she came through.

"Wait," she said, smiling. She had a little dried blood on her lower lip. I didn't see it until she smiled, and I didn't remember hitting her. Lee Ann disappeared downstairs, returning with eight bottles of Rheinlander, the cheapest beer available in the state, as far as I know. After a struggle, she managed to get the bedroom window open; she pushed the storm window open, lined up six beers in the windowsill, and closed the inside window. Instant bedside beer fridge.

She opened a bottle for me, the lid dropping to the floor and rolling under the bed. "To your last day of work flipping burgers," she said. "Cheers!"

Lee Ann could brighten up your day like that. I was back from the brink. She'd taken a cold, gray winter day and let me see the beauty of the newfallen snow. Traffic hadn't even blackened it yet.

"Cheers," I agreed.

"I think we still have some acid in the fridge," she said. "Wanna get lost today?"

I shrugged, happy. "Doesn't look like I'm going to work."

She said, "Not in weather like this." We clinked our bottles together. Things were looking up.

Lee Ann

Lee Ann was not a small girl. She wasn't real, real fat, not really. She just had some extra. Big hips — birthin' hips, my old man would have called them, but I hadn't seen him in seven years, so him seeing her to call her hips birthin' hips didn't seem very likely. Good-size tits. She smoked Marlboro Reds to spite her folks and keep the weight off, said she gained 15 pounds the last time she tried to quit. A weird little nob of a nose. She was the kind of girl people call "almost pretty."

Tough times. I couldn't make enough to both get loaded and pay the bills, so I did what I could to game the system: juggled bills, waited for winter to come so I could stop paying the utilities, turned off the stereo and kept quiet when the landlord came knocking. But Shitty always slipped us a few freebies among the beers we ordered. That helped us stretch the dollars.

Now I remember what the fight was about. Lee Ann hated rubbers. Said neither of us could feel anything with one on. So she'd taken to demanding a few lunges without one. She started out cautious — "Come on, just one," then "only a couple," and so on. But the count had gotten high and I was telling her to get off me, pushing her away, and she just kept holding on. She finally started hitting me. It was like she was possessed. Or maybe I hit her. Yeah, I think that might be how it went — I think maybe I hit her first.

I'm pretty sure I came while we were fighting. Man, I wasn't happy about that. A shadow from our little game of Russian Roullette and its consequent fight was still with me that next morning, but like I told you, Lee Ann just had a way of making things look up.

We dropped a dose to fuel the new day and toasted the new coat of snow over breakfast.

Rat

Man, we loved breakfast. When things were booming along at bar close, the party usually came with us, back to Dodge Street. With the most sincere apologies, Shitty would send us out into the night with promises to catch up. The Fox Head's 20 minute bar-time lead let us stumble into Dity John's Grocery, just across the street, and grab the supplies we'd need to keep the bash alive. Then a drunken trudge home, through the snow. The cold didn't matter to us — we were impervious by that time of night.

Shitty would find his way to our place, a case of beer and any other intoxicants he might want to sell in tow. Shitty had a funny habit: He'd dose, crack open a beer, and — and you could almost set your watch by this — 45 minutes in, he'd suddenly experience the grave need to wear my steel-toed combat boots.

"Hey man, can I wear your boots man? Just tell me where they are," he'd say, the look in his eye anxious, worried that I might say "no," or that I might have lost them. I'd never told him "no," but you know how urgent things can seem when you're like that. Once he had on the boots, everything was smooth sailing and clear skies with shitty. He'd have a grand, drunken trip with us, a glittering voyage through late-night infomercials. We had a favorite: The vacuum-pack guy, this chubby guy who sold a machine for bagging things in custom-size plastic bags, then vacuum-sealing them. Shitty always snuck off to our room and fell asleep on our bed, wearing the boots.

Ah, those nights with Shitty and Lee Ann and Larry at the Fox Head! I feel like I could live inside such great times forever — just crawl back into one of them and lock the door behind me.

Or maybe that was the night Larry exploded out of the kitchen in a shrieking gallop, barely keeping himself upright and yelling, "Rat! There's a fucking rat in the kitchen!"

It was mid-December. Larry's prematurely gray-brown, shoulder-length hair was all over the place. I don't think any of us believed him. I certainly didn't. But you know what psychotropics can do to your judgment.

We decided to mount an expedition, Shitty, Lee Ann, and I. Larry stated emphatically that he was not venturing down the hall until we'd got the rat out. We advanced slowly, wary of our enemy, each of us now sunk deep into the LSD. Shitty brandished a heavy ceramic ashtray. I wielded a copy of Hustler from Larry's stash, rolled up into what I thought of as a weapon. Lee Ann clutched the back of my shirt in both hands. Who knows how long it took us to reach the kitchen? Not I.

The long and the short of it is that we found no rat. We did, however, find rat shit in the box that held an unfinished Paul Revere pizza no one could remember ordering. It had been out for a few days, and a couple of discarded syringes nearby gave me a pretty good idea why no one recalled the pizza episode at all. Lee Ann had left Shitty's place of employment before bar close earlier that week. I thought nothing of it — I'd just decided it wasn't time for me to turn in yet. So I went through the motions: drinking with Shitty at one end of the bar; picking up more on the way home; trudging through the snow to the dive on Dodge, passing Lee Ann's '72 Lincoln in the front drive. I don't remember seeing the Paul Revere's box then, but the lit candles and lack of electric light on in the place as I came in confused me. Then I spotted Larry and Lee Ann going at it face to face on a dining chair in the kitchen, needles discarded with belts nearby. They'd been shooting heroin.

I think I should have been angry. I think a guy's supposed to be when he finds something like this. But I wasn't. It was just a smack fuck, I knew that. Didn't mean a thing. It was just the kind of thing you did on smack. They'd probably turned off the lights to minimize the glare; I'd seen the light from the usual electrical bulbs go all streaks and haloes on smack, but mostly it did the opposite, just left your pupils scrunched down into tiny little pinpricks. The effect on heroin is so strong, Larry and Lee Ann might have thought they were hiding in the dark with the lights low like that. As I recall, I took the drinks upstairs with me to give the two of them a little privacy. I didn't want to embarrass anyone. They just hadn't noticed how late it was, is all. But would it have killed them to have saved me a taste?

Anyway, back to the rat. Larry, hands clutched in his long, knotty hair, demanded that we destroy the beast. None of the rest of us particularly wanted to kill the poor creature. I for one could think of no other solution. Then something clicked for Shitty. He was on board.

"I'll need my .22," he said, and with considerable authority. He suddenly sounded like a big game hunter, a man's man on a sport-killing safari. Like he was looking to tangle with the world's most dangerous predators right here in our kitchen.

Firing a gun in the kitchen while we were all dosed to the nines did not seem altogether wise to me.

"Come on, Shitty," I said, "it's all the way across town."

Shitty stared at me in defiant incomprehension for a second or two or whatever, then deflated a touch. "Poison," he said.

I shrugged, raising my hands and shoulders. We didn't have any rat poison. Why the hell would we keep rat poison around?

"We must venture to Econofoods," Shitty intoned. "They'll have the poison. They're open 24 hours. They're the place." Shitty would take the reins of this trip and guide us to our goal. We would have our kill.

Shivering from the drugs and with Larry whimpering quietly to himself, we decided, two hours into our trip, to strike out into the cold, snowy night for Econofoods. I kept thinking to myself, "Focus — *focus!* If we're going to drive on LSD, one of us has got to focus!"

Only I must have been saying it out loud; I noticed the others looking over at me, alarmed.

"Nothing," I said quickly, "nothing at all. Don't worry. We're doomed if we worry ... "

And so on.

Larry's little powder blue car, a weathered '76 Nova, would be our chariot. Our chariot with frozen locks, as it happened. But Lee Ann had lock de-icer. We were still in business.

We were hallucinating great wobbling ripples crashing over the road, all of us were. We decided to put our heads together, all of us but Larry, who seemed to have gotten one of his hands tangled in his hair, now. He really did not seem able to free it. Lee Ann stared, wide-eyed at him for a long stretch, then burst out laughing.

"What?" he asked. "What?"

Shitty and I looked questioningly her way, but she was laughing too hard to speak.

In huffing, heaving bursts, she said, finally, "His hair! His hair — it's a *rat's nest*. Get it? Where'd the rat go? I think I know where that rat went."

I understood. Acid logic. Or acid humor. Whatever. I smiled and nodded at her in what I hoped was not a condescending way. Larry, his slight gut over his belt as he sat staring at her, said nothing. He was wearing a stained white button-up with faint vertical lines of tiny roses. I never could get a handle on Larry's style. But that didn't matter. He was a good friend.

My license was expired, but I was the only one of us who had one at all. So I sat behind the wheel. My cohorts decided to help me navigate. They told me they'd try to arrive at a consensus on which way I should steer to avoid the really big waves. Their pupils dilated and eyes open wide, they would be the extra sets of eyes I needed to make the journey.

It was a little hairy. The snow was fresh, and hid sheets of ice in unpredictable places on the road. We hit one (I think) and spun Larry's Nova into a snow bank sideways; then another put us into someone's front yard a few feet. But between the car and our pushing, we were able to get it back onto the road and soldier on.

"The rat," Shitty kept repeating. "The rat!" I think he was making some kind of mantra with all that repetition.

Things went on like that, pretty much, until we slid into the nearly empty parking lot. I think we were going about seven miles an hour. The night shelf-stockers were out recovering shopping carts. That looked like hard work; the shopping carts weren't really designed to handle snow of any depth, and there were a few inches out there. The night stockers stopped to watch in wonder as Lee Ann told me to head one way, then Shitty the other. I think we drove around out there very slowly for a while. Not that it seemed slow to us. But the way the stockers stopped everything and gawked, they could see that something was amiss.

We almost lost the Nova when we finally agreed on a suitable parking spot; I forgot to put it into park, and as we stopped to get out, the car started to roll. A heroic dive from the back seat, and Larry's free palm was on the brake, his legs awkwardly up over the seatback.

"For God's sake, put it in park," he was yelling. He kept repeating himself while we tried to figure out how to reach around him and hit the gearshift. But between us, we got the job done.

Big Box

I don't know if you've ever been inside one of those big-box groceries at a quarter to four in the morning, but we had. Only we weren't tabbed that time last summer. At least, the last time I'd made the trek at this time of night, I was merely stoned. With maybe a snort of speed to keep me sharp. Then a couple of shots of Kentucky whisky to take the edge off that. During the summer, they'd keep their big entry doors wide open, and birds would sometimes fly in and kind of get stuck in there. Lee Ann and I had come in search of eggs and potatoes and cheese and sausage, that sort of thing, breakfast stuff, and you know how stoned people shop; our cart was filling up with stuff we had no use for. The Econofoods was like an airplane hangar, huge and hollow, its ceiling lined with fluorescent tube lighting. The electronic buzz the lights made was awful, and the light deeply unnatural.

Lee Ann noticed the sparrow flitting around overhead, pointed it out with a gasp of wonder.

With a loud crack from a few aisles over, the sparrow exploded, its body bloodied into a new shape by buckshot. We could see that as it fell, with a thump, next to a cooler with rows of bloody ground chuck, the really low-grade stuff. We heard a sound like hard rain coming down around us. The little steel pellets were shooting down on us in the meat section. I covered up and ducked down, but Lee Ann, not understanding what was going on, stood, gawking, until one caught her left eye on the rebound.

I think maybe the people working overnight in the place thought there weren't any customers around. Otherwise, why would they be shooting guns indoors? Someone could get hurt. Watery red trickled from where the little pellets punctured the ground chuck. It was like some kind of canned hunt, in its way. That chuck didn't stand a chance.

Lee Ann had closed her eyes for a second to clear them. The pellet that nailed her struck just beneath the brow of her eye socket. Man alive, could that girl scream. I loved to hear that shriek of hers. The night manager came running over with a look like he'd been caught spying on a junior high school shower room.

"Oh my god, oh my God," he kept saying.

Lee Ann was shrieking at him, "I'm gonna be blind, you dumb motherfucker, I'll blind you, you stupid cunt, see how you like being blind," helpful things like that. She was kicking and clawing at him. It took the other four night stockers on duty, pale, sleepless guys who shunned the daylight, to wrestle her away from him. The night manager told us then that we could get what we needed and go, the store would cover it.

There it was again: Lee Ann's weird ability to get a bad thing looking good.

We combed the aisles then, genuinely chipper, Lee Ann holding a cloth with some ice cubes wrapped in it to her eye, grumbling obscenities. But the grumbling was just for show. She'd flash me a smile, sneak one at me when she knew they weren't watching. With $13 between us, we loaded down the cart, then retrieved a second and filled it to overflowing, too. We stocked up months' worth of food. Too bad it was so late; you can't buy alcohol in Iowa after two.

Rat, more

Lee Ann's eye puffed up black and blue, and people gave me dirty looks on the street when we walked around together, but she was fine.

But that was another time, before. This time was the time with the rat.

The four of us trudged past the night stockers in the parking lot. They were having a hell of a hard time getting the carts to roll through the snow. But they'd gotten back to work; must've seen enough of our show. I bet you see lots of weird shit on the night shift at a big box grocery.

The electric buzz and awful pallor of the light struck us, but we steeled ourselves.

"We are on a mission," Shitty declared, "to make your house free of rats and thus safe for Larry."

All eyes ogled over to Larry, whose hand was now clearly inseparable from his knotted nest of hair. You could see the light go on in Lee Ann's head. The thought balloon over her head read loud and clear: *Rat's nest!*

She giggled. "Come on," she said, taking Larry by his good hand and leading him away. Shitty and I followed.

Lee Ann went aisle by aisle until we found a suitable pair of scissors. When she was sure the coast was clear, she popped the staples holding the paperboard sheaf together.

"Oh no," said Larry. "No, no, no, you are not cutting my hair in the fucking Econofoods at four in the morning."

I checked my watch. "Three forty-seven," I said. Larry glared at me. "It's just in the name of accuracy," I said. He returned to Lee Ann.

"Look," she said, a nurturing, maternal tone appearing magically, "your hand's stuck. We have to get it free. Looks like there's a bunch tangled up in your rings, everything."

The slow shift in his expression told me Larry was being won over by something about what Lee Ann was doing or saying, and while my mind went off on its own, trying to discover what it might be that was winning him over to her, she started cutting. Big tumbleweeds, snags, and whorls fell at our feet, and Larry's hand slowly came free, the wings of the bats on his three enormous heavy metal rings snarled in sandy gray-brown coils.

He looked pretty bad. Lee Ann took off her ski cap and pulled it down onto Larry's head.

"Poison," said Shitty. He was not going to let the purpose of our visit drift away on us. We combed the aisles until we ran across what looked to be a suitably deadly bottle. I couldn't really read the dancing letters, but the skull and crossbones seemed enormous. With drug-impaired difficulty, we found our way back to the front of the store and bought our prize. How would we ever find our way home if we couldn't find our way out of the store?

Homeward Bound

On the way home I suddenly saw too many springing headlights in the windshield. We swerved across the center line. I remember the blur of an oncoming station wagon. Time turned to molasses on me, molasses in which every detail seemed crystal clear, no matter how tiny; I had time enough even to analyze it. The inertia must have been incredible. I felt my neck pop, then pop again as it jammed to the side and was held in place with the force of the spin. After what seemed like hours, the force eased up on my neck and we came to a rest and I realized that my face had smashed into the steering wheel. My nose and brow were numb, but I could taste the copper and feel the wet warmth running off my chin. We got out to look the Nova over, see if she was still roadworthy. Shitty got a look at me and pulled a handkerchief from his coat pocket, handing it to me. He showed me where to press. Larry, poor Larry, was knocked out, but breathing in the back seat. Shitty and Lee Ann seemed unharmed. The front end was bashed in pretty good, but I thought we could make it before the police got there.

Then I noticed Lee Ann staring, pointing down the road. Four people were sprayed out glistening across the road, bodies I thought probably, pretty well skinned on the pavement. The wagon was in the ditch at the side of the road, its headlights cockeyed.

"I didn't even see them," I said. She reached over to grab onto my arm and suddenly I was screaming, my vision whited out by the pain.

"I think it's broken," she said.

I glared at her. No shit it was broken.

The headlights of another car appeared at the curve. I could see the curve, now, that the wagon had come around. The oncoming car wouldn't see the other people.

"Come on," I said, urging the others toward the Nova. But I couldn't seem to will myself to move. We could all see that the oncoming car would not see the people on the road, that that would end any question of their death, and not one of us could look away.

The oncomer was a Chevy Conversion-style van which, truth be told, was going a bit too fast to be safe. Its driver locked up the brakes after destroying the first victim, but still managed to plow into the others. They never had a chance.

"Holy shit," said Larry, rubbing at his eyes. "What the fuck just happened?"

We limped homeward with our rat poison and our injuries, the Nova randomly, flickeringly lit no matter what we tried to turn out the lights. I couldn't drive with my arm like that; Larry had to.

"Back there," said Shitty pointing past the end of the drive, into the secluded back yard. "Way, way back." Larry went along with the order, though he didn't seem happy to be leaving his car snowbound. Lee Ann let herself into the basement we could only access from outside, like the one at Dorothy's farm in "Wizard of Oz." When she climbed back up and out, she was carrying a tarp.

Inside, Shitty produced a vial of clear fluid from his coat pocket. "I was saving this for a rainy day," he said.

"What've you got?" I said.

"Morphine. You're going to shoot up. Then I'm going to set your nose. I've been in enough bar fights to handle that. But the arm — the arm worries me."

"Dude, I cannot handle this, I cannot watch this," said Larry. With a fumbling grasp, he picked up the rat poison and headed for the kitchen. Lee Ann, her face ashen, sat motionless.

"You should go with him," said Shitty. "You don't want to see this."

The funny thing about morphine is this: It does not dull your pain so much as dull your capacity to care about it. It's a lot like clinical depression that way, I'm told. A dose of morphine and you don't care what's on TV, as long as the TV is on. The nose hurt like hell, especially when Shitty had to try it a second time. But the arm. Thank God for the morphine.

I was laid out on the floor by now. Shitty stood over me. He folded a washcloth over on itself until there were lots of layers. "Open your mouth," he said. He carefully placed it between my molars, as far back as he could wedge it.

He took my wrist in his hands, braced a foot under my arm. "Guerilla medicine," he said with a screwy smile. There was a limb-tearing jerk on my arm, and my world became only the sound of my own muffled scream and the gunshot-wound pain of my arm. I flickered out.

When I came to, I could hear the others talking strategy. Well, OK, it was more of a reinforcement of the collective decision to never, ever mention the crash to anyone. Lee Ann had taken out my hair clippers and was leveling what was left of Larry's hair into a flattop.

I closed my eyes and submerged into narcotic darkness.

Breakfast

That was the worst hangover I'd ever had: a home-set broken nose; a home-set broken arm in a sling we'd made from an old sheet; the acid hangover crackling at the edges of everything; the alcohol hangover, with the asphalt-scarred feel it brings to your ass and innards; the neck still sore from the spinout and the rest; and the post-narcotic funk. And God, we'd killed people. I was miserable. I was sure we'd get caught.

But taking the party to our place meant one thing: Hospitality. Even if we had no money, even if we were hung over half a dozen different ways, by God even if we'd run from a fatal collision in which we were most likely the cause, we'd prepare breakfast for whoever had stayed. Today's menu was typical: an omelet-scramble of a dozen eggs; however much milk seemed right to Lee Ann's intuitive gaze; onions and green peppers chopped in the kitchen by Lee Ann or me; and topped with Mexican Style Velveeta, the cheese-spread with hot peppers and other Mexican stuff in it. We'd scoop the breakfast scramble onto a bed of hash browns from the freezer and melt the Velveeta and serve Jimmy Dean breakfast sausages on the side.

Lee Ann smiled at me over the food as it cooked through. Her look said one thing to me: All in all, things were OK. No one had died — none of us had died, anyway, nor even suffered a life-threatening injury. That was amazing! God, did I hurt, but she was doing it again: Somehow, even through all this, things seemed to be looking up. If you just looked at it right.

The Good Life, Pt. 2

The Rheinlander bottles in the window, that was a couple of weeks before the time with the rat. That was a stroke of genius. No shit. We stayed in bed for a few extra hours that morning, only getting up for aspirin, or to take a leak. I only barfed once, and it was a small one, no big deal. I did it to myself, sneaking a little hit of smack in the bathroom, away from Lee Ann, so she wouldn't know I still had any around. I didn't even mention it, just gargled my mouth out with a swig of beer. I made sure the phone was off the hook. No need to take calls from Burger King if I didn't work there.

Man, were we happy. I played music on the radio and Lee Ann stripped and sang along with Springsteen, but only a few lines, and with a huge smile: "*Well lately when I look into your eyes, I'm goin down ...* " but she left out the parts of the song that were about a burnt out couple tired of each other and doing one another more harm than good, their love melting down into hatred, both setting each other up *just to knock-a knock-a knock-a* each other *down, down, down, down.* She gave me a blowjob to that song to celebrate my last day at Burger King, and ignoring the pain of the bruises she'd left on me, I thought to myself: *Y'know, life is all right.*

Miles was in to open the Fox Head at 11:30, usually, just before the lunch rush. We didn't even need to change course to avoid Burger King. That was off our beaten path. It was cold — winter mornings in Iowa are like that. So we bundled up, no big deal.

But the Fox Head was not open when we arrived, and it was something like 12 degrees out, far too cold to wait around outdoors. So we decided to wait in Dirty John's Grocery until we saw the *Open* sign light up.

After a while — I wasn't wearing a watch — Lee Ann started getting antsy. As she gnawed impatiently at a fingertip, a little old woman behind the counter seemed to take a suspicious interest in us. Lee Ann was not amused. Her hands had begun to shake, just a little. Nothing just anyone would notice. I was pretty sure it was just the LSD, not DTs; she didn't do all that much smack, really.

She turned to me. "Jesus Christ, why can't we just go over to the bar and get a seat?" she said. Her voice had taken on an angry edge. She turned and glared at the woman behind the counter. "What?" she demanded. The little old woman started, surprised. Lee Ann and I had been drinking for a couple of hours and were now otherwise medicated, and while I hadn't seen a reflection of myself, I could see it all over her: dark circles under sunken eyes, creases tracing the weariness around her eyes and mouth.

With an irritated huff and dismissive, stabbing wave, Lee Ann stalked away from the old woman. When she thought she was out of the woman's sight, she scooped a fifth of whiskey into her bag.

The little old woman said, "Is there anything I can help you find?" Her voice was full of worry — she probably didn't much fancy entertaining a couple of junkies already at it at this time of day — but she asked.

Iowans. You just gotta love Iowans.

I think that the woman might have seen Lee Ann shoplifting. She certainly could have, with all the security mirrors set up around the store. But she let Lee Ann walk out of the place with no hassles. I looked at the store's clock on the way out, smiling apologetically at the woman. It was 12:15. Other people had walked by the Fox Head, peered in, and moved on. We decided on George's, another bar only a block away. I'm amazed it didn't occurr to us before then, but we just usually didn't hang out there.

We trudged through the snow of unshoveled walks between us and George's.

There were customers at George's, probably a bigger crowd than otherwise, had the Fox Head ever opened for lunch. As we pulled off our layers, one by one, Lee Ann drove a fierce glare into me. This wasn't going to be good. The storm that was Lee Ann Russo was about to come ashore.

"Don't!" I whispered.

But she was past that point. Her voice climbed to a shriek that turned every head in the room. "You worthless sonofabitch, can't keep a job, even a shitty job, won't defend me when there's old ladies looking me up and down like I'm a thief or something!"

God, I loved that scream. But this was public. This was embarrassing.

"Where you folks been drinking earlier?" asked the bartender, a wiry thirtysomething man with stringy, colorless hair and the smoke-stained look of tavern life about him. He seemed familiar, somehow, though I couldn't place him.

"Oh, uh," I said, "just, y'know, at home. And stuff."

He shook his head *No* at me and walked over. "Sorry," he said. He addressed me by name. "Another day, maybe. But I can't have you two in here like this right now."

Lee Ann gave me a look trembling with rage, willing me to act, her expression delivering the message: Coward. Loser.

I guess by that time my reflexes and reaction time must have been down. I did take a swing at the bartender, but he just sidestepped it and slugged me. I know I went down. It didn't hurt much, really, but it numbed my cheek and knocked me over. Can't imagine how much that would've hurt if it'd happened in the days after the crash.

Lee Ann bitched and moaned all the way home. About a block from the police station she laid into me about the burger job again, and again, and again, and I just let one fly, doubling her over. A second too late I realized how dangerous it was to have done that right out here, in the open, in the daylight, near a police station. This was the kind of thing you kept private. But no police came. We were lucky.

The rest of that day is a blur of misery and intoxication. I remember watching something on TV. I remember the awful gray light of winter seeping in through the blinds. I remember laying low. When I heard a truck pull up outside, I knew it was Bobby Earle's rusted once-white '67 Ford pick-up. I peaked out the side window and sure enough, there he was, eyes glassy and unfocussed, dirty blonde hair unkempt and spraying out from under his Lorsban cap, a thermal vest on over a flannel stained with engine fluids, his moustache struck through with frozen snot. It was, indeed, my landlord. I recall Lee Ann seeing him once.

"Where'd he ever get the money to buy a place — even this place?" she said.

"Inherited," I told her. I'd heard about people getting something for nothing and not giving a shit about it. So it was with poor inner-city folks who were handed new homes in so many failed projects. So it was with Bobby Earle and the property left to him by his long dead daddy. Bobby Earle didn't need a job; but his daddy, seeing what his money was doing to Bobby, stipulated in his will that the estate was to provide Bobby with an allowance, the house he lived in, and the house we rented. That way, Bobby couldn't get at all the money at once to squander, I guess, and would still be taken care of. And his allowance was evidently enough for him to get by on, seeing how infrequently he actually seemed to try to get the money out of us. In exchange, though, we didn't dare call to have him fix anything. When the downstairs stool backed up, it pretty much rendered that room unusable.

Bobby drank very heavily, had shots with whatever he bothered to eat for breakfast. By the time of day when he started wondering about the last time he'd got rent from us, he was usually blind drunk. Not hard to fool him. He knocked unevenly for a few minutes; I saw his silhouette pass on the other side of the drawn living room curtains.

Then muffled cursing, boots crunching on snow and gravel in the drive, and the engine of the '67 turning over. Bobby Earle wouldn't try again today.

My internal clock was so messed up I fell asleep at 4:30 or so. When I woke up, the clock said 6:45, and it being dark out, I didn't know whether that meant daytime or night.

I cracked open a capsule of speed, cut it into two lines, and snorted them. Lee Ann was nowhere to be found. Least, not at the house.

I found her out at the Fox Head with Larry and Shitty, very, very loaded. Shitty was sitting pretty close to her, and I thought maybe she'd hit the end of the line with me. But she turned to face me, streamed smoke from her nose and mouth, through a beaming, mood-swung smile, and I knew everything was going to be all right.

Shitty turned to see what she was looking at. With a smile that hesitated for a hiccup, he waved me over, cigarette dangling from his mouth. "Dawn of the Fucking Dead, man, where'd you come from?"

He clapped me on the shoulder and pulled a mug from the fridge behind the bar.

Larry looked nervous, too, like the three of them had been caught at something. I did not care. Truly I did not. I let Shitty pour me a beer and used it to wash back some more cheap speed. There was music on the jukebox, a noisy crowd having drunken fun on a cold winter night, and I didn't know what day it was. Honestly, no idea. The cigarette smoke was so thick I didn't even have to light up. I felt like a gypsy. It was like surviving by picking what you wanted to eat from the apple trees as you walk pass, or from someone's garden. Things were looking up.

That's the thing about those nights: They weren't all that bad. We'd hit some rough spot, then Lee Ann would make all the bad just kind of drift away, even if she'd caused it in the first place. "Lee Ann says you were out pretty hardcore," said Larry.

"Yeah?"

"Yeah. She told us she shook you and shook you, but you were dead to the world," he said.

Huh. Never had any idea she tried to wake me. But then I thought maybe she didn't, really; maybe she just had to get away from me for a while. I don't know.

I don't know how late it was when everyone fell into their spots around the house, but Lee Ann fucked me somethin' special. It was still dark out. I told you about those le cheval voodoo possessions of hers. They were getting longer. I thought maybe she didn't give a fuck about consequences, or maybe she thought a kid would make everything right for us. A lot of people make that mistake. I don't know. But I had to fight her pretty hard to get pulled back in time. She tore up my back with her nails trying to hold on.

When she was off and I was holding a clenched fist over her, blood running down my back, she glared at me, locked eyes with me. She gave me a few seconds like that, then pushed past me. Through the open door of the bathroom, I could see her digging at the skin under her nails with the lid of a bottle cap.

Our Kind

After the crash, damn, did the cold made my broken arm ache. I didn't have it in a cast, but Shitty'd set it, and we'd hung it across my chest in a makeshift sling, a loop of old bedsheet tied around my neck. The pain you get when you move a broken arm the wrong way teaches you fast.

We putzed around the house, stayed fucked up most of the time. We all agreed it'd be best not to be out and about in a small town sporting injuries that made us look like we'd been in a car crash, not while the fatal wreck was still being looked into and was fresh on everyone's mind. My black eyes slowly faded from swollen and purple, to less swelled up and a kind of brown-beige mottle. Shitty and Larry brought us drugs and booze. Twenty days into it, Lee Ann and me were stir crazy and in need of other company. I tried out my arm free of its sling, and it didn't seem bad.

"Whaddaya think?" I asked Lee Ann. She was an amphetamine blur twitching her way along the seams of the house. I tried to tell her that speed was not the way to go when you needed to kill time, but —

"HellYesLet'sGetTheFUCKouttaThisHellHole," she said. Her eyes were glazed over, wet and distant, dilated. She shook. She glowered mercilessly at me, my black-mood baby. She blew past me, shoving against my hurt arm, and it didn't feel broken anymore, but the shove left it a little sore.

When we turned up at the Fox Head, Shitty looked like the sun just rose at his door.

"Guys!" he said, smoke gusting around the cigarette in his mouth. Shitty's teeth were ringed in stains that I presumed to be tobacco; it looked like eyeliner for teeth. He kept a full, brushy beard during the winter months. Shitty pulled a Marlboro hard pack from the pocket of his red-and-black flannel and shook some toward us. We took him up on the offer. Someone put a Joplin tune on the jukebox.

While we sat, smoked, and drank, Shitty caught us up on what we'd missed, which was pretty much nothing. Once or twice I saw Lee Ann making eyes at some young, clean-cut guys in a booth across the bar. I'd never seen them in the place before, hadn't seen them come in, but then, my back was to the door. I decided not to notice her making eyes. She could play flirt if she wanted. We were in this thing together.

The jukebox said, "*Oh Lord, won'tcha buy me, a Mercedes Benz?*"

Sitting across from Shitty with Larry someplace nearby, it felt so much like old times I forgot Lee Ann's mood. God damn, can that woman's mood swing. All at once, out the corner of my eye, I saw her glaring straight at me.

"You don't care," she said. "You don't care one bit about me."

"Now, Lee Ann — " I said.

"Three weeks in that fucking coffin of a house with you ... "

"We had to, honey. We — "

"Almost got me killed in that wreck — " Her eyes smoldered angrily at me, her lips pulling back from her teeth in a clenching snarl.

That set off Shitty, who wanted no one talking in his bar about any fatal wrecks he'd had anything to do with. "Lee Ann, for fuck's sake, pipe down," he said, his voice a hoarse whisper.

"God-damned murderer, that's what you are, a god-damned mass — "

I didn't feel it coming. Her words had turned sour on me so quick I didn't even know she'd pissed me off. But she had. She'd crossed the line. And before I knew what I was up to, my elbow'd connected with her nose, knocked her off her barstool onto the floor. Blood streamed from her nose and mouth and she bawled, angry at the blood, angry at the world, angry at me.

Shitty said, "Look, you gotta get her outta here, I can't have you two in here like this."

I felt a deep, subterranean pain in the arm I'd broken and which I'd just nailed her with, the right. The break had been just below the elbow, and I obviously hadn't seen a doctor or anything, but I was at that moment pretty sure if I had, he wouldn't have advised me to hit things with it just yet.

Shitty was around to our side of the counter now, got us each by an arm and walked us outside. "Seeya next time," he said, smiling and nodding. He deposited us on the walk out front, turned, and headed back in, shaking his head.

The clean-cut guys spilled out, three of them, and the one who she'd been batting her eyelashes at came straight at me. I put up my dukes, but I usually lead with my right, and I'm not much of a fighter to begin with; having to stop and rethink how to lead with the left instead stopped me dead long enough for him to double me over with one to the gut. A boot or a fist or something caught me on the forehead and down I went, scraping my hands in the snow and sand and salt.

Then, in the quiet dark of the night, I heard Lee Ann shrieking. I looked up to find her on top of the clean-cut, looked like she'd jumped on his back from behind. She was howling all sorts of crazy shit at him about having to go through her if he wanted to hurt me, her husband with the broke arm anyway, what the fuck did he expect, the big tough man, like that.

Imagine that: Her *husband*.

In amazement, the clean-cut ducked and let her just kinda slide off him, over his head and onto the ground.

"Crazy bitch," he said, shaking his head. "Crazy bitch."

He turned and waved his cohorts along. "Let's go. Fuck these people. Lowlifes."

"We didn't want you down here, anyway!" The shriek again. After a second, she added: "We don't want your kind around here!"

Lord, did I love that shriek. Who could resist Lee Ann all fired up like a bag full of bobcats? Not I. I stuck out my left hand, a peace offering, and helped her to her feet.

Lee Ann looked around in a daze, turning slowly around, around, around in the snow. Her eyes came to rest on a nice, well-kept house down the block. A family home. A good place to live. It was two floors plus attic, an exterior that looked to be made of some kind of big gray bricks. There was still a Christmas tree lit in the window, though we'd laid low and stayed high through the holidays, and hadn't put up anything like that, didn't have anything like that.

Lee Ann wandered toward the big, stately structure, her mouth gaping.

"Look at that place," she said. We could see a woman in a house dress sitting at a table with a man whose shirt was the kind that looked like it had had a tie on it earlier. They were smiling. We could see two clean, glowing kids in the window, passing a bucket of rolls we knew were fresh and hot. We knew that because that was what would be right, the right way to do things. And this was one of those families that did things right just because that was the right way to do things. I'd never met a family that did things right just to do them right. A happy family gathered together at the dining room table for a square meal. The man of the house didn't even have a martini. I realized that

I must have thought it was later than it was. But the scene was a sight to behold for the sheer, Norman Rockwell, Saturday Evening Post cover normality of it. A sight whose picture-book normality stirred a burning shame somewhere deep down inside us both.

I usually kept such visions from my mind with a kind of mental game of tag. If such ideas never tagged me, I wouldn't have to worry about them. But to keep the ideas at bay, I had to be aware of them, had to live right at the edge of that truth: That I and Lee Ann were not that kind of people — that we were another kind.

Lee Ann had begun to cry, softly now.

I put an arm around her — cautiously, but I did. "What's got you down, baby?" I said.

She couldn't seem to *not* look at them. She just stared.

Very softly, she said, "Those people — why do people like them get to have what they've got? Why don't we get to have what they have? Why don't we get to have a nice, warm, fixed-up house, and a nice family, and a nice dinner, and nice, happy children ... "

She suddenly looked like she'd put on 20 years. Her stare broke from the family, slipped down the walls of the house, down the yard, to her feet. I couldn't see her face then, but the tears fell to the cold ground.

Lee Ann snatched up a rock and flung it at the house with everything she had. It struck the gray brick of the side wall, didn't hurt anything. I was so caught off-guard I couldn't even think of what to say. She dropped to her knees, grabbing up more rocks, then lurched to a teetering upright and started raining gravel down on the house.

She said, "That's not true! That's not true! That's a lie — that's a goddamn lie!" like someone was trying to pull a fast one on her.

A light came on over the front door. I don't remember what I said, but I had to do a kind of running tackle, scooping her over my shoulder to get us outta there.

When we got home, we found a note from Bobby Earle's lawyer, threatening us with eviction if we didn't contact him and pay up to current. Our time on Dodge was running out.

My arm took a few more weeks till it stopped hurting so much. But a cold snap always made it ache. Damn. The morning was dark, overcast even more than usual for February in Iowa. Lee Ann was crying when she woke up. I was just rubbing at my arm, absentminded, didn't even hear her at first.

"Plate," I thought she said. I reached out to her, finding her in the darkness. My tongue tasted like a skid mark, and I in no way recalled coming to bed. I coughed my throat clear, felt around for a smoke.

"What's that, baby?"

"I said," her voice harsh, "I'm. Late."

A haze went over my eyes as I thought of all the things we could do to get out of it. There was always some way to get out of it.

"A baby could fix everything," she said, and her eyes were dreamy all of a sudden, and I thought of the dreams that must be flickering behind them. A baby room in our house. A wicker carriage. The white dress she'd wear on wedding day. The more I thought about it, the less likely it all seemed. The house wasn't our house — not really. Sooner or later, and probably sooner, Bobby Earle would be by to kick us out. I was often surprised that he hadn't done so yet. I'd let the grass go all summer last summer. Finally mowed it when the city stuck a complaint notice to the front door. That grass was nearly four feet tall, and still no sign of Bobby Earle. I think he missed the whole thing.

But Lee Ann was feeling good this morning, seemed happy enough for the size of the problems we found ourselves saddled with. I wasn't about to interrupt that. It was my time to make sure things kept looking up.

The Good Life, more

We needed out. The only thing keeping us from homelessness was Bobby Earle not showing up, and he was going to come knocking at the house sometime. That note from Bobby's lawyer and Lee Ann's and my last fight had sent Larry away with his bags to a one-room walk-up across town. We were the only ones left, and we didn't have any money for rent. For anything. It was good luck that we'd never accumulated much in the way of possessions. Otherwise, my plan of action would've never worked.

All we had in the world fit into three duffle bags. Lee Ann's road-weary Lincoln, expired plates and all, was enough to get us to the Days Inn practically next door, in Coralville, just off I-80.

The clerk gave us a look, and I guess we did look a bit washed out, but things were starting to look up. The hotel wouldn't ask us to pay up until it was time to check out. When that happened seemed to be up to us.

Our new home was dee-luxe. It had a bedroom with cable, a desk, and a dining table. A semi-separate kitchenette next to the table held a little fridge and microwave and a Mr. Coffee. There was an indoor pool. Lee Ann and I dined on room service burgers some nights, delivery pizza others. We'd get beer at the Hy-Vee down the road, then pour a couple into plastic coffee travel mugs, snap down the lids, and take them down to poolside, to the hot tub. One morning we met a guy who was traveling through on business, wound up at the Coralville Days more or less by chance. A secretary in his office chose that one because it wasn't as pricey as the hotels in Iowa City. Said he was there to sell paper to a printing plant south of town. A traveling paper salesman? I'd never heard of such a thing.

I told him me and Lee Ann were students who were between leases, riding out the time. He laughed.

"In college I guess you can do things like that," he said.

We laughed, too, nodding and sipping beer from our mugs. These were good times. We were living the good life, a jet-set hotel lifestyle. Everything was new and clean and worked.

We walked into the lobby, microwave meals and cold Milwaukee's Best in tow from the Hy-Vee, on our twelfth morning at the Days. The clerk cleared his throat at us to catch our attention. I walked over to the counter.

"What's up?" I said.

He looked around like he might get caught talking to us or something. "The manager said to have you two pay up," he said.

"Ah," I said.

"I thought I'd let you know before he came knocking on your door."

"Ah. Well, now, I appreciate that," I paused to look at his ID tag; "Jerry. I really do much appreciate it."

Lee Ann and I rolled everything into our duffle bags and our grocery bags and loaded up the Lincoln. We wanted to stay in the area, because a little townie tavern called Billy's had grown on us and we wanted to be able to walk there. We set down about three blocks from the Days, at a small motel called The Sunflower Inn. The Sunflower was an older building made of big cinder blocks, painted white, a strip of individual rooms sharing walls, side by side. There was an outdoor pool, but it wasn't late in the year enough to use it. But all that didn't matter much. We'd found another place to stay. Lee Ann just kept smiling at me, happy to have me showing her the good life. She talked about quitting smoking. I wasn't interested, but kept that to myself.

Our fifth night at the Sunflower, the time seemed to have arrived. We watched cable with our beers until sunset, then walked down to Billy's. I ran a tab and made like a big spender. We drank like there was no tomorrow, smoked our way through three packs. When we'd put back enough beer, I ordered a round of Wild Turkey shots. Then, with Lee Ann giggling drunk, I ordered another. I cracked open a capsule of Benzedrine and, while she was visiting the Ladies' Room, stirred it into her beer. I added the contents of a capsule of blue cohosh. Then another. An herb expert at the little hippie store told me it was just the thing. I stirred her beer again. I don't even remember how many I bought. But I remember paying the tab with a check. We could go to Billy's one more time, maybe, before they were after us for that.

I woke to Lee Ann gasping and sobbing. She was throwing up in the bathroom. She must have felt awful with all the toxins we'd pumped into her together at Billy's. There was a wide, wet red circle on her side of the bed. And I tell you, despite a pounding hangover and a sense of impending diarrhea, relief swept over me.

In the bathroom, I cradled Lee Ann's head, running my fingers through her hair.

"Don't worry," I said. "Nothing's gotta change. Don't worry. You'll see." Things were looking up. 'Cause see — it was my turn to do it. My turn to get things to looking up again for her.

The Helvetica Story

"The Helvetica Story" first appeared in the journal Eleven-Eleven, Issue 15, August 2013.

I heard about Helvetica. What a story! As a child, all the print-journalism fonts used to bully him.

"Snub nose!" they'd sneer.

Often, he would find "GET SOME SERIFS!" on typewriter paper epoxied to his school-locker door, in the telltale script of his tormentors: Times and his cousin, Times New Roman. The Times cousins often brought Courier with them to heckle Helvetica. And Courier was a good enough guy, actually, but a bit dull. They only brought him along because he took up so much room.

It was frustrating, being harassed by fonts that had been around since hot-metal typesetting; it was no secret that exposure to that much lead early in life caused learning and behavioral disorders, so what was he supposed to do? He didn't want to get a reputation for picking on the slow kids.

The calligraphic fonts did their worst, looking askance down their lavish swoops at him, but they're so tight-kerned you couldn't pry a needle from their ass-cracks with a tractor.

Still, it all took its toll, chipping at Helvetica's self-confidence day-in, day-out. Discrimination against the sans-serifed continued to plague him, leading to a misspent young adulthood of sex, drugs and rock & roll. He went out to nightclubs on the prowl, and he got around, littering the town with offspring he'd refuse to acknowledge — Arial, Futura, Univers — but the lineage was no secret. They were chips off the sans-serif block. Anyone could see those vertical and horizontal strokes from a mile off.

When the computer age began to dawn, the people he was contractually bound with began demanding exorbitant licensing fees. To spite them, he renounced the name he was known by commercially. He became "the typeface formerly known as Helvetica." He started calling himself \—/, which was irksome, because as far as anyone could tell, it was unpronounceable. "Artists," they said, shaking their heads.

But it bore the clean lines and straightforward angles that were his calling card, and the fans still recognized him.

He went around wearing caps with bills as camouflage, and jackets with epaulettes, to blend in among the serifed. Then he went to work on his skin, tattooing on whirling tribal patterns, flowing sickles and curlicues to mask the bland, smooth lines he always found staring back at him from the mirror.

In those dark days he hung out in the clubs at night with the twin goth typefaces Morpheus and Mason. The Avant-garde fonts were part of that whole scene, and got \—/ (nee "Helvetica") hip to new modes of expression through his art. He discovered that he had a knack for photography. His still images captured the majesty of the hot- and cold-set presses of yesteryear. These were well-received in small, bohemian galleries, but eventually he discovered that he had access to a greater range of expression that the additions of motion, sound, and lighting afforded.

And then \—/ had moment of clarity, a brilliant beam of light striking his imagination from another place: Gone were rules suggesting that a typeface must be set in stone — or in lead, or on a printed page, for that matter. His first use of the new medium was to change the rules, conceiving of an ever-shifting, animate font. His creation would be one wherein parts of each character would be showcased separately by its own, individual lighting, rotating at its own rates and angles. In this new medium, he found harmony between the serifed and sans-serifed that he had always found missing in his own life. A watchful eye would capture the transformations: At times each section of each character had its serifs, but those flourishes would fade as people watched, to cycle back again. He called the concept font *Animalgam*. (It even made Prototype, from the edgy Virus Fonts, jealous to have been crafted in such a static format!)

He unveiled Animalgam as a gallery installation, a high-definition, ever-shifting animation, when along came a man, a designer who would become a thief, who'd come to desperation and nearly to suicide with his own inability to inspire a client. Admittedly, this was a big client, and this job would make or break one's reputation in this business. And this client had become impatient.

The thief, whose name does not merit mention here (why give him further fame, even if it is infamy?), pilfered Animalgam to satisfy this big-ticket client. The client was a 24-hour news channel whose executives wanted to add an edgy design element. They commissioned a logo so distracting that viewers wouldn't be able to pry their eyes from it. Thus was Animalgam stolen.

Of course \—/ never saw a penny for it. And he felt robbed. He did.

But he had had the troubled youth of one bullied for being different; the days and nights spend off the map, hanging with goth and industrial types, and even those crusty-punk corroded fonts, Vintage Typewriter and the other worn-down fonts. He'd even hung out with Gill Sans, though not for long; certainly Gill Sans had been sleek and perfectly legible, even from a distance, but his unsavory paraphiliac obsessions, particularly concerning his own children, found him quickly demoted to *persona non grata*).

While \—/ was out of the spotlight, imitators stepped up, trying to claim his spot. A boy band of look-alikes appeared with corporate sponsorship. Its lineup:

- Helv, by Microsoft;
- Monotype's CG Triumvirate;
- Paratype's version, Pragmatica;
- Bitstream's Swiss 721; and
- Nimbus Sans, from the type designer URW++.

But, like the group of look-alike / dress-alike / James-Dean-hairstyle-alike musicians hired to back Morrissey when the Smiths called it quits, the fans knew that they were not interchangeable – not quite, anyway – with \—/.

And others – always others. He saw his reflection as he walked downtown one afternoon and thought he's gained some weight, until he realized that he was only see Helvetica Rounded, just out for a stroll.

When the boy band broke up, his corporate sponsors renamed Helv *MS Sans Serif*, rebranded with their corporate identity and with the rise of the Web, ironically enough, MS Sans got most of the attention for a while.

That was the arrival of the Internet age, and with Windows the dominant operating system, MS Sans was everywhere. But the new age brought another surprise: On-screen, the serifed suddenly looked awkward. Chunky. Clumsy. Probably not very smart, and certainly not very stylish.

The new media shined a hard light on the serifed, and found them pixelated and wanting.

Into this new era, \—/ awoke and, his old name now spreading, knew that it was time to reclaim his title and emerge into the spotlight once more. His re-emergence demanded a makeover that would impart sophistication, maturity, perhaps a whiff of something European. Thus did \—/'s Neue (*new,* in German) persona arrive.

the reflecting pool

"the reflecting pool" first appeared in Hotel Amerika Issue 8.1, Fall 2009.

6.8   josh sommerford gazes into the swimming pool, its surface glassy, reflective, its floor glittering pool of water and sunlight and glass, and time pooling, pooling, in the pool. their pool: that of josh sommerford and josh sommerford's wife, teema; their pool. but it has seen better days. electrically-luminous, drying leaves scuff along the poured concrete in the early autumnal breeze. a skin of dead insect chitin roofs one corner.

1.1   when josh and teema first met, he was certain that the fates must have planned their unlikely meeting in time and space, specifically during their undergrad years at iowa, working in hair nets, bulky, starched-white uniforms, and under tube lighting, at the unfortunately-named burge food service. burge. purge. regurge. ick.
this is the earliest of their moments; it is the earliest of the reflections.

1.2   he can see it all as though it's playing out before him; he reflects upon the reflections in his reflecting pool, his and teema's, reflecting the moments — their moments, vivid as the original. meeting her, stunned with her beauty and vivacious energy, teema *teeming* with life! hair nets and bulky starched things and all, but his vision cut through all that to find him stunned by her beauty. in a *hair net!* imagine.

6.9+ 1.2   ~~he can see it all as though it's playing out before him;~~ he reflects upon the reflections in his reflecting pool, his and teema's, reflecting the moments — their moments, ~~vivid as the original~~. he's not well, our josh, we can see that. his hair is unkempt, the scotch from last night fouls his first-thing-in-the-morning breath, to which he is adding only coffee. the effect is a taste on his tongue, the taste and texture of a skid mark on pavement. he hasn't shaved in a few days — not long enough to seem to be in active pursuit of a beard, merely unwashed and hardscrabble; he looks like shit — because, who's gonna care, right? besides, there are no more mirrors in the house.

x.1   all these moments, reflected …

6.4   he sometimes sees himself reflected, sometimes a few years younger, healthier, hair cared-for and beard kept in check. happier times, these, with josh, and josh with teema. he can see it in his eyes in these moments: he felt preposterously lucky to have her, had hardly believed when, after working with her for seven months, he finally worked up the courage to ask her out. he can see that gratitude, see it reflected in his eyes, reflected in the pool, these early, happy moments.

6.5   other times, he sees himself toward the end of their time — his and teema's time — together. if he cared about himself, he would not like what he saw. but he no longer cares. he first noticed the reflections in the pool a few days after teema left, packed up her prius and their dog, boris the borzoi, and, like a wrecking ball to his gut, drove away, boris grinning his canine grin, tongue lolling, as he watched through the rear window and the prius pulled away. pulled away forever. dumb damn dog. josh does *not* feel like joshing. he is, instead, devastated. teema is the love of his life. he cannot come to terms with the notion that she will be absent from it from here on out.

2.1   the swimming pool (josh sees as he reflects upon their lives together) has become the epicenter in their lives. she has become a poet of that rare, publishing kind, and teaches poetry classes part-time at a local college; and he has a dull but well-salaried position documenting an internal software project for at&t in new jersey. the two fling themselves into their new professional lives, gathering a circle of good friends and their families, and begin hosting parties 'round the pool. people bring beer, wine, floaties, kids. it quickly become a community, these people, these drinks, this pool: everything revolves around the pool that summer. everything —

4.2   — at first they do not react to teema's withdrawal from the festivities.
the gatherings, in fact, do go on —

x.2   all these moments, reflected …

y.1   all this light, pooling …

note 1.1   sometimes, an object can accumulate an extraordinary weight as a story progresses, can become the black hole about which the story orbits, accumulating meaning, waiting to one day, perhaps, suck in the rest of the story, bring it crashing to its demise. Think, *e.g.*, of hulga's wooden leg, in flannery o'connor's "good country people."

3.2   josh sees himself joshing around the pool, sloshing a bit of gin and tonic on the poured concrete surrounding it, he wearing one of his trademark pairs of mirrored sunglasses from his oddly large collection of them. "don't fall in," teema cries, but she's laughing as she does so. and, josh sees, there's that look again in her eyes: a happiness, a wonderment, a vibe. she retreats to their kitchen and returns with a fresh pitcher. boris trots about, the people sneaking him little slurps of beer, tongue lolling through the middle of that borzoi grin — not the smartest of hounds, but a happy one.

6.1   josh is wracked with abandonment, betrayal, dumped, left to die, at this end of the spectrum. teema is gone, and boris the borzoi with her, packed up and left to her parents' home in iowa. teema has left. has left him. teema has. he gathers several pairs of discarded mirrorshades from the previous eve, hurls them to the concrete, and stomps on them. lenses fly. he tosses them into the pool; the mirrored lenses spark up at him from the pool floor. it strikes josh as having an odd, shattered beauty to it. and as this notion strikes him, he catches a moment, a flash — something passing across the lenses. *what the — ?!* he gathers more of last night's glassware from around the pool and begins a rain of shattering glass down upon the pool's floor, a sparkling, electric shower of light captured, however briefly, in slow-motion descent, repeating luminescence through the transmarine atmosphere, a shower of sparks and glints and shards of light.

x.3   all these moments, reflected …

y.2   all this light, pooling … a static rain of phosphor and moments, water and glass and light … a labyrinth of moments …

6.6   and josh sees them: the moments. his moments — their moments together — playing out across the shattered mirrorscape of the pool. these moments, these everyday happinesses, that he thought had disappeared forever, gone down the road toward iowa with the dog, he sees them … sees

1.3   — their moments, vivid as the original. a lifeline to these happinesses, these scenes.

6.9   josh fears that if he leaves the reflecting pool, the reflecting will stop. ah — there's the first date, his mistaken impression that a guy friend she knew might instead be a boyfriend, the awkwardness on both sides as he and teema worked up the courage to try some expression of affection, a hand-holding, a kiss, even, maybe, maybe … . josh feels a panic: he can only see the scene in fragments. vivid fragments, but a patchwork of reflections in the pool, in the shards. he wants it — wants to relive it as fully as he might. into the house he runs, to the kitchen, to the cupboards. he carries glassware out, the long-stemmed ones, the no-stemmed wine glasses, and begins shattering them into the swimming pool, shower after tiny, isolated squall of sparks and memory and light flickering down through the water. out come juice glasses, the blue-glass goblets, the red-glass snifters, and shattering, down they go.

x.4   ~~all~~ these moments, reflected ~~…~~ across the pool's surface and its floor.

y.3   all this light, pooling … a static rain of phosphor and moments, water and glass and light … a labyrinthine, luminous pool of reflections …

1.4   there they are. josh can see them reflected in the hurricane of glass and lenses on the pool's bottom: their moments, reflected in a dizzying, dazzling labyrinth of light: a car he can't afford to ferry him to and from her parents' home across the state, in des moines, that first summer. they spend time together, skinny-dip at a local country club after hours, scaling a low fence and shedding clothing, excitement piqued with the risk. he sees the two, naked in the pool, reflected in his own pool and its reflective glass gazing ground. he can reach out — he can almost touch it … almost …

7.1   at one end of this stands josh, no job, no degree, no pool, but he's just met a girl. her name is teema. at the other end stands josh, older, broken, stopped making it to work so the degree isn't much use, a gazing pool full of sparks and moments, glittering, electric moments, vivid as the original, and no girl named teema. but he has the pool. he is afraid to leave its side now, afraid the reflections will stop, and he'll be left without her forever.

x.5   hairnets … first date … first jobs … a beautiful, happy, if not very bright, russian wolf hound … the pool … the people round the pool, the entourage … life that summer in orbit about the swimming pool …

3.1   he glimpses the parties: their friends, their friends' kids, boris the borzoi, gin-and-tonics all 'round, big band music alternating with underground music brought along by the male members of this group, this entourage, in an ongoing competition to out-hip one another, the music swimming out from the house, their house, his and teema's. their entourage beginning to arrive shortly after five, just after clocking out, and, hell, they're friends, so josh and teema show them where the spare key is kept, just in case that godawful central jersey, north-south traffic ties one or both of them up. the gatherings must go on!

3.3   drinks slosh on the poured concrete. tipsy friends occasionally play up their tipsiness, tumbling into the swimming pool in full dress; that gets a laugh every time.

~~he can see it all as though it's playing out~~
~~before him;~~ he reflects upon the reflections
in his reflecting pool, his and teema's,
reflecting the moments — their moments,
~~vivid as the original.~~ he's not well, our josh,
we can see that. his hair is unkempt, the
scotch from last night fouls his first-thing-
in-the-morning breath, to which he is
adding only coffee. the effect is a taste on
his tongue, the taste and texture of a skid
mark on pavement. he hasn't shaved in a
few days — not long enough to seem to be
in active pursuit of a beard, merely
unwashed and hardscrabble; he looks like
shit — because, who's gonna care, right?
besides, there are no more mirrors in the
house.

he can see it all as though it's playing out
before him; he reflects upon the reflections
in his reflecting pool, his and teema's,
reflecting the moments — their moments;
vivid as the original. he's not well, our josh,
we can see that. his hair is unkempt, the
scotch from last night fouls his first-thing-
in-the-morning breath, to which he is
adding only coffee. the effect is a taste on
his tongue, the taste and texture of a skid
mark on pavement. he hasn't shaved in a
few days — not long enough to seem to be
in active pursuit of a beard, merely
unwashed and hardscrabble; he looks like
shit — because, who's gonna care, right?
besides, there are no more mirrors in the
house.

1.x: reflective, reflected

6.7   josh sommerford gazes into the swimming pool, its surface glassy, reflective, its floor glittering, a coherent pool of sunlight, and time pooling, pooling, in the pool. their pool. josh sommerford; josh sommerford's wife, teema; their pool. but it has seen better days. ~~electrically-luminous, drying leaves scuff along the poured concrete in the early autumnal breeze~~ leaves brown with death have swirled into one corner, and dead mosquitoes ride the waves nearby. ~~breeze.~~ leaves brown with death have swirled into one corner. a skin of dead insect chitin roofs ~~one corner~~ another.

4.1   the entourage, you see, come to admire josh and teema, this ideal-seeming young couple, recently married and still shining like a honeymoon, come to idolize their marriage, see it as an example of how best to go about the business of lifetime partnership. that radiance, that clear affection, drew the entourage into an orbit around them, each friend alight like a tiny nova, luminous, alive. they could never conceive of life after work that summer, around josh and teema and boris and the glimmering pool, as finite, endable, mortal. these moments were their moments, too. which is why — at first — they do not react to teema's withdrawal from the festivities.
— the gatherings must go on!

4.3   they want to ask what's wrong, what's bothering teema, the first day of her withdrawal. they want to, but they do not. they want to on the second day, too, and so on, but because bad news about josh and teema would be a heretical thought, they do not ask him, and she does not appear.

0.4 everything begins to zero here —

6.2   and josh begins to see them: ~~the moments. his moments~~ — their moments together — playing out across the shattered mirrorscape of the pool. these moments, these everyday happinesses, that he thought had disappeared forever, gone down the road toward iowa with the dog, he sees them … sees , horribly, himself: disheveled, unshaven, skin flaking, hair a stalled hurricane of dandruff.

6.2, addendum   he can't stand the sight of himself, his ruinous face a reflection of the lives he's ruined, a reflection of the ruin he has wrought upon himself, the ruin he has, himself, become. he roams the house, smashing mirrors and tossing the shards into the reflecting pool.

0.3 everything begins to zeroes here —

x.6   all these moments, reflected …

0.2   everything begins to zeroes here —

0.1   everything zeroes here —

0.0   everything zeroes here — moment zero —
josh sees her, reflected in the shards of light and reflection, a mirror of shattered glass and transmarine, see the look on her face when she realized the truth.

x.7   all these moments, reflected …

4.4   — the gatherings must go on!
the gatherings, in fact, do go on —

5.1   the entourage keeps the fire burning, keeps the gatherings going, though a few raise eyebrows when teema's prius isn't in the driveway one day when they arrive, and thereafter does not return. they keep bringing the beer, the drinks, the so-hip mix cds, and themselves. but then josh stops coming out to the pool, as well.

4.5   — the gatherings must go on!
the gatherings, in fact, do go on —

4.6   someone leaves an old fedora on the kitchen counter, near the screen door, so everyone can pony-up for things like paper plates and plastic glasses. what the hell? they have the spare key. they clean up after themselves diligently. but after a few days an unease creeps into the entourage — for who are they entourage to, if both josh and teema have withdrawn?

4.7   — the gatherings must go on!
the gatherings, in fact, ~~do~~ don't go on —
they peter out as the members of the entourage begin to contemplate the heretical: josh and teema have had a falling out. the last of the die-hards calls it a season when josh, who has been out of sight these past few days, suddenly reappears, litters the pool bottom with the shards of the house's glassware and all of the reflective lenses from all of his sunglasses, and takes to falling asleep in a lawnchair by the pool,. he is not well, our josh; he hasn't shaved lately. his hair a blizzard of dandruff, always about in the same pajamas and robe, all sliding toward ruin. he can't stand the sight of himself.

x.8   hairnets ... first date ... first jobs ... a beautiful, happy, if not very bright, russian wolf hound ... the pool ... the people round the pool, the entourage ... life that summer in orbit about the swimming pool ...

> and teema's voice, like winter wind across razorwire, a sound so sharp and crystalline it threatens to shatter in to a blizzard of tiny, blazing crystals of ice and fire: "why the hell would you *ever* do this to me?"

... finished. in the reflection of the reflecting pool, josh sees the tale-end of his time with teema. her name is ghislane, she works with josh, and when teema finds the hotel receipts there is no consoling her. josh, unable to admit the scope of his sin, simply returns to the party. for a time, anyway. teema does not.

7.2   the whole of it has become a much, much narrower passage than before; he can only go

back as far as meeting
her, and never makes it
past the first reflections in
the pool. at the far end
stands josh, no job, no
degree, no pool, but he's
just met a girl. her name
is teema. at the other end
stands josh, broken,
stopped making it to work
so the degree isn't much
use, a gazing pool full of
sparks and moments,
glittering, electric
moments, vivid as the
original, and no girl
named teema. but he has
the pool. this is all he has
left now; it is the last of
their moments — the last
of their reflections. he is
afraid to leave its side
now, afraid the reflections
will stop, and he'll be left
without her forever.

x.9   all these moments, reflected …

note 1.2   sometimes, an object can accumulate an extraordinary weight as a story progresses, can become the black hole about which the story orbits, accumulating meaning, waiting to one day, perhaps, suck in the rest of the story, bring it crashing to its demise. think, *e.g.*, of ~~hulga's wooden leg, in flannery o'connor's "good country people."~~

josh and teema's pool; it is a finite pool, a gathering of shards, moments, and light, shattered glass and mirrors, hairnets at one end and unkempt psychological ruin at the other: the end of their moments, all swirling now in the far corner with the leaves, brown with death, and the chitin bodies of the season's mosquitoes.

32 FT/Sec^2

"32 Ft/Sec^2" first appeared in the Journal of Experimental Fiction, Issue 39, January 2011.

1.1b   damon's life flashes before her eyes: playing doctor with janet, the girl who lived down the block. wondering, now, what has her life been like

1.1a   lorraine's life flashes before his eyes: the drought that year during her childhood when the spiders went crazy, webbing anything and everything they could, and how spectacular and terrifying all of that gossamer silver thread was, wafting in the breezes, draping from every outdoor surface.

3.1   the inexplicable sense of heartbreak and loss when his first girlfriend who, at age 12, he barely knew really; how could something so small actually knot him up inside?

9.1   her husband returning from world war ii, a war hero — her *husband!*

2.1   falling —
            moments flashing —
                cascading —
                    but this is not normal time, it is brain time
                        and it is nearly at a standstill ...

0.2   he is falling through the air now. nothing can stop that. he's taken the leap.
        falling
            falling
                falling

7.1   the american dream: a small cottage on adams street, in a young neighborhood; the life-giving joy of a family that rapidly grows, two, three, four, five, six, seven, eight; the horrible death of the soul that a stillbirth bring to the couple: the injustice, the inversion of time represented by parents burying their child.

4.1   his job as a copy editor, his fluency in four style manuals, and *webster's dictionary of english usage*, which none of the other, more seasoned editors had even heard of, his pride at being one of the vanguard who watch over the english language. late nights working for a morning newspaper, later nights, occasionally, as the night editor, the one who sticks around after the paper's put to bed, waiting to proofread the first copies as they roll off the press.

10.1   jim — her *husband!* — a sizeable man to begin with — gains weight over the course of their years together; she feeds him well the rest of the week, and on sunday, she feeds the extended family pot roast with mashed potatoes, stewed veggies, and buckets of gravy. jim retires from his car-delivery job at 65, right on time, and, with a growing sense of uselessness, tumbles into a slow cycle of despair and, two months to the day after retiring, dies of heart failure, leaving lorraine to settle the details, the remains, of their lives together. working with her children, she finds an apartment within a retirement home, and settles in to a schedule: card games monday night, big band music from the '40s and '50s on tuesdays, wine socials thursdays and saturdays, etc. she is enjoying a glass of wine in the peace of a seat on the screened-in porch of her apartment —

5.1   meeting damiana there, of all places: at the news desk. they worked together well into the night of august 31, 1997, an evening that began with a bulletin over the newswire around 4:30:

news alert*news alert***news alert*** /
princess diana in car accident. broken arm.
more to follow.

and the two of them looking at each other, knowing that a broken arm would not provoke a news alert like this, that — they both knew it — something bigger was happening. — and learning a few hours later that diana was dead, and that a slow news night had suddenly become something no one working the evening shift would be escaping anytime soon. and the following morning, the two of them greet sunset at his place after work for a drink, the newspaper having become an all-night project, rather than getting off at the usual midnight punch-out time. and that being the beginning, as the moments passed and neither moved to end their conversation, and they realized something was happening between them.

6.2   — to take a flying leap from the retirement home across from ~~their~~ his apartment

2.3   falling —
        moments flashing —
            cascading —
                but this is not normal time, it is brain time
                    and it is nearly at a standstill ...
                        a nearly immortal moment
                he will fall, eventually, but for now, his thoughts and hers swirl in one another's minds

8.1   and lorraine's war-hero husband taking over the finances, cashing the checks, meeting his war-hero buddies at the legion hall saturdays, returning home with precious little of it remaining at the end of the day. and their fights over the finances, her screaming at him, demanding that he take better care of his children and not drink his paycheck every saturday. and their children filling the small house past capacity, the two adding bunk beds in the second bedroom and more in the basement. and the children growing up and one-by-one, attending columbus high school, the city's catholic high school, and, one-by-one, the children graduating and moving on to find jobs. the 60s were well afoot by now, and the children, one-by-one, found jobs or, in the case of the oldest boy, went to fight in vietnam.

2.2   falling —
        moments flashing —
            cascading —

but this is not normal time, it is brain time
and it is nearly at a standstill …
a nearly immortal moment

3.2   the ~~inexplicable sense of~~ **crushing, inescapable** heartbreak and loss when ~~his first girlfriend who, at age 12, he barely knew really; how could something so small actually knot him up inside?~~ damiana was, pointlessly, torn from him in a wreck with a pick-up piloted by a man who was swervingly making his way down highway 35 from austin's sixth street bar circuit. it was weeks ago — months; why can't he shake the sense of horrifying desolation?

and lorraine's husband, jim, slowly coming around, slowly spending fewer days at the legion hall, slowly bringing more of his paycheck home to the family. and the two of them, empty nesters now, watching the first of their grandchildren arrive, and the presence of children's laughter in their small cottage again, after so many years.

0.3   he is falling through the air now. nothing can stop that.
        falling
                falling
                        falling
        hurtling earthward at a speed approaching 32 feet per second, squared

0.1   when his eyes —
        when her eyes —
                meet hers.
                meet his
                        and they connect, form a circuit,

0.0a   fuse. they are locked in now, he in hers, she in his. he is falling. nothing can stop that now; he's taken the leap. but this moment, this exists in its own kind of time: it exists in the mindlocked space of brain time, their neurons firing at the speed of light, compared to which 32 feet per second squared is a syrupy, crawling pace.

feet per second squared is a syrupy, crawling pace.
mindlocked space of brain time, their neurons firing at the speed of light, compared to which 32
now; he's taken the leap. but this moment, this exists in its own kind of time: it exists in the
0.0a   fuse. they are locked in now, he in hers, she in his. he is falling. nothing can stop that
(from his perspective, she realizes, she'll seem upside-down, though he's the one who's wrongside-up …)

6.1   their wedding, the wedding of damon and damiana, planned and scheduled for three months out, a date mocking his loss from its marked spot on the calendar that hangs in the kitchen. he is out with the other editors after finishing up one night, when it happens: a friend of one of the women he works with comes home with him afterwards, because when you get off work at midnight, two a.m. seems pretty early, and they sleep together. in the morning, he feels like a monster, subhuman, because although damiana has been gone for months now, he still feels, burning at his core, a sense that he has betrayed her. he cannot stand his own company. he considers the worth of life without damiana, and he decides —

4.2   his job as a copy editor, his fluency in four style manuals, and *webster's dictionary of english usage*, which none of the other, more seasoned editors had even heard of, his pride at being one of the vanguard who watch over the english language. late nights working for a morning newspaper, later nights, occasionally, as the night editor, the one who sticks around after the paper's put to bed, waiting to proofread the first copies as they roll off the press.

0.3   he is falling through the air now. nothing can stop that.
falling
    falling
        falling
hurtling earthward at a speed approaching 32 feet per second, squared

2.4   falling —
    moments flashing —
        cascading —
            but this is not normal time, it is brain time
                and it is nearly at a standstill ...
                    a nearly immortal moment, **stretching on and on**
he will fall, eventually, but for now, his thoughts and hers swirl in one another's minds, **when she decides that she's staying right where she is: in his headspace.** *forgive yourself*, **she thinks to him, and in the next instant: fission will occur, a separation; and damon will taste cabernet on his lips.**

0.x   ~~he~~ **she** will fall through the air ~~now~~ **at that moment.** nothing can stop that. **but that moment has yet to arrive. and it is the current, nearly immortal moment with which we are concerned.**
    not falling
        not falling
            not falling —
    not hurtling earthward at a speed approaching 32 feet per second, squared.

Calling

"Calling" first appeared in Gargoyle literary journal, Issue 62, November 2014.

We laughed at the Judeo-Christian myth of the Great Flood, the one about Noah's Arc — laughed and shifted our gazes back to our smartphones. I mean, did we *really* want to embrace a story whose consequences would include the entire human population being hopelessly inbred? We needed to log back on.

The Noah flood myth even had historical precedent; Suasanna reminded me of that once. The Mesopotamian *Epic of Gilgamesh* includes another such deity-wrought, world-cleansing event. The flood myth in the *Epic of Atra-Hasis* pre-dates that; that one's another tale of the divine summoning a deluge to punish humankind.

We laughed, back then, before the calling began, compelling people to leave us.

Not everyone; we don't know why some are called, others not — or perhaps, just not yet called. No, the calls come on no particular schedule, compelling some — though none below the age of 16; we have no idea why — to leave us behind and follow the summons. The first calls led their victims into the waters. The first walked into the Mississippi. Then came the Gulf of Mexico, the Mediterranean, the Atlantic. We live in an age of declining sperm counts worldwide, yet our technology allows our population to march on past the 7 billion mark. I cannot help but wonder this: Could nature manifest in some form to deliver these calls?

Then the cries began calling women into the vast cornfields of the Midwest.

The summonings seem to come from beings of yore, sea and river and forest nymphs, wild, mythic creatures embodying aspects of the natural world — a natural world that is reclaiming its place from the technology-saturated one we built.

The Summoned ones who are called into the Mississippi take on a distant look before they yield. They begin, long before they finally yield to the calls, to reek of mud. We find dirt and twigs in their hair.

The Summoned who are called into the oceans also fall into disengagement with the world around them, our world, though they began to smell of salt air and seaweed, a fishy sort of scent. Their hair begins to bleach, and their skin reddens, as if from windburn and sunburn. Then they tan, though none need venture out into the sunlight for that to happen.

The Summoned who are called into the cornfields begin to smell of dirt and hay and manure; maize pollen dots their hair and their clothing, seemingly from nowhere, before they succumb and leave. Their hands and arms and faces become chafed, as if by the coarse sides of corn leaves. And they, too, show signs of wind and sunburn and unprompted tanning.

Somehow they all slip away into the wild; we never see them again. Which sounds impossible — I mean, no matter how vast the cornfields of Iowa seem, they're finite. We should be able to find them and at least try to rehabilitate them. But no — they're gone; they simply vanish.

So yes, we laughed — until the Summoned started to vanish. What got me puzzling about what it is that is actually going on was when my fianceé, Suasanna, fell prey to the call.

I began studying those flood myths, looking for answers.

The Norwegian version is about the sea swallowing the city of Saeftinghe. As the story goes, Saeftinghe was technologically advanced and prosperous to the point of extravagance. A mermaid somehow became trapped in the city's wellspring. Different versions of the tale are out there, but in this one, the mermaid pleaded for help; when the people of Saeftinghe laughed and ignored her pleas, she declared that the sea would rise and swallow the city. And, in 1584, the sea did just that. Saeftinghe sunk below the waves, its advances and achievements reclaimed by forces of the wild. Saeftinghe was a real, historical city, and it really was flooded in 1584; the sunken city is known now as *Verdronken land van Saeftinghe* — the Drowned Land of Saeftinghe.

I wonder: Are our people being called away because of some wrong against beings who live in the oceans, the fields, the rivers? One of the Summoned, as she tried to resist being called into the Pacific, said that the voice calling her wailed incessantly about the rain of garbage from its sky — from our world — a deluge of trash and excrement that began when humankind began to cross that body regularly. That plaintive song has a point; I mean, have you seen how vast the Pacific Garbage Patch is? A swirling gyre of plastic and rubbish stretching from off the California coast, to Hawaii, all the way to China and Japan.

As I dug deeper, I found flood myths woven throughout many cultures throughout the world: The Ki'chi and Mayan peoples had theirs, as did a number of First Nations peoples in the Americas. The Muisca people, and the Cañari Confederation, both in South America, had similar tales. Ziusudra is listed in the Sumerian Kings List as the last to rule before the coming of the great deluge.

In South Asia, the Hindu Puranas include such a story in the *Satapatha*
Brahmana and *Matsya Purana*. In Plato's *Timaeus*, Zeus brings a flood to punish
humankind.

Again and again, human cultures around the globe recount tales of vast,
destructive deluges. Massive torrents washed humanity's influence from swaths of New
Orleans, then New York, the ecosphere reclaiming territory more aggressively when the
slow reclamation of Venice did not deliver the message that we were going too far,
tainting the whole world with our technology and its byproducts. But did we stop?

And then there are the supposedly mythical mermaids. Did a mermaid's spurned
cries for freedom doom Saeftinghe? Could sea nymphs, or creatures something like
those, be calling our people away, into their embrace?

Ancient Assyrian legends tell of these seagoing people, and sightings continue to
be reported even today. Christopher Columbus claimed to have seen them as he
explored the Caribbean, and today, fish-men sightings have been claimed in Canada
and the Mediterranean; creatures of this sort have supposedly been sighted in every
ocean and sea, and even some of the great rivers.

And mermaids are historically associated with the sirens, shipwrecks, and floods.

We have evidence in the form of hair samples from Africa that have been tested
and proven to be from a previously undiscovered great ape. Mongolia has its *almas*, or
wild man. Rangers patrolling Way Kambas National Park in Indonesia claim to have
witnessed dozens of tiny human-like people, bedecked in dreadlocks and wearing no
clothing. Are all these creatures — avatars of the wooded wilds — reaching out to

remind us that we and our technology cannot exist without the hidden worlds on the fringes of our civilization? The gods of the old world rising again?

I have given up on maintaining my yard; it grows so quickly and so thick that my lawnmower can no longer cut through it. Thick moss has overrun the sidewalk and driveway.

Something is happening — and now, it is happening to my Suasanna.

I barely noticed, at first. When she became slow to respond to e-mail messages, I thought little of it. But then she pulled the network cable from her computer and smashed the connector ends with a brick. Her cheeks, I noticed, took on a bit of color, as though she'd been out working in the yard, somewhere where she'd gotten some sun.

I was alarmed when she stopped using the computer altogether, and more so when she put her smartphone in a drawer and locked it. She won't touch the thing anymore.

On my way home, I passed a hairy, dirt-smeared man with an enormous sign that read, "THE END IS **NIGH**!" He was shouting something about us all putting science before the gods.

Suasanna started to smell of seaweed, subtly at first. Now the fishiness is almost pungent. She won't touch anything electronic.

"I can feel it," she said. "The call. It's trying to drag me away."

"But we're engaged," I said, as though that would make the compulsion go away.

She turned, eyes swirling a transmarine-aqua toward me. "I don't want to listen," she said, "but the glaciers, the ice floes — "

"Fight it," I said. "Resist." I'd seen the panicked reports streamed on our broadband connection. Something is happening, and we do not grasp what it is. For whatever reason they are chosen, those who are called all succumb, eventually. But her breath was already frost and fog. She sits naked now, eschewing clothing as unnatural. Occasional patches of flaky ice appear, seemingly at random, across the canvas of her skin. The arctic. The arctic is what's calling to her.

I repair to the garage for the bungie cords I keep in the trunk. When I return to her, she has not moved. I use the bungies to tie her down, secure her, keep her from falling victim, becoming one of the Summoned. To keep her.

In England, women begin to speak of the fairies calling out to them. In Iceland, they say they hear the elves singing out from the distant, cold, wild countryside. All over the world, science is losing its battle with a resurgent, seemingly magical influence. Antibiotics fail; a common influenza has become fatal.

I gaze out the window toward poor Topliff's house; like so many yards formerly meticulously manicured, his has begun to grow with such speed and ferocity that he cannot keep pace with it. It almost looks abandoned, now, overrun by plantlife, some of which has not been seen in these parts in decades. His wife left last month, after abruptly sprouting a thick coat of hair across her body and emitting a strong, earthy, pine scent. The Pacific Northwest woods had summoned her.

When I turn back to Suausanna, her chair is empty, save for the bungie cords; only a few scattered flakes of ice remain behind, already melting away.

Waterloo Talking

"Waterloo Talking" first appeared in Rivet: The Journal of Writing that Risks, Issue 1, Summer 2014.

Hughes Avenue in Waterloo, Iowa, was not a new street, and not in a new neighborhood even back then, but with so many kids arriving on the scene, so many young mothers and so little traffic, the concrete seemed more like a playground, a surface suited more for children than for cars. That's where we lived, we Farbens, that mid-'70s summer: In the house on Hughes Avenue where my mother had grown up. She'd hang laundry out on the line and white sheets that had flapped in the wind for a few hours would come back fresh as the breeze.

It was the first time that word had ever come between us, and it tore open a fissure between David and I that we never managed to make right.

We'd steal a flower from the riot of unchecked growth in old "Auntie" Agnes' yard for our mother. If we only took a single flower, and only once in a while, and then only from the blossoms that pushed out over the sidewalk, through the black iron fence surrounding her raised, terraced yard, she never seemed to mind. Fritz never did.

Fritz was Auntie Agnes' dog, a barrel-chested monster mutt who, whatever else was in his pedigree, showed clear signs of German Shepherd lineage. But there was more. Fritz was bigger than any Shepherd we'd ever seen, and his hair, though short, was a riot of shades and tints. Alongside a

German Shepherd's browns, blacks, and golds, Fritz had streaks of blonde and tan and red slashing through his coat. Fritz loved us neighbor kids. He'd draw his hulking form to the edge of the fence and, with a cautious, delicate whine, ask for our hands and attention.

My family never really had much money; my mother dropped out of high school when she became pregnant with me at 17, and my dad worked construction.

For us, brotherhood arrived unexpectedly: Black and my age, David's parents became traffic fatalities on Highway 20 in a fiery head-on collision during a thunderstorm. A pickup coming the other way misjudged the slickness of the roads and hydroplaned smack into them. My friends and I wowed each other with the ghoulish details we conjured of the scene, envisioning the carnage through the lens of our imaginations: The driver of the pickup hadn't been wearing a seatbelt. Had he launched, a human torpedo bursting through the windshield and into the car carrying David's parents as they returned from dinner at a Cedar Falls restaurant? Did they all burn to death? What did that *smell* like? We imagined the whole thing like an action movie, the same collision viewed again and again from different angles.

That sort of speculation died off when David came to live with us. No one could bring himself to ask another child, especially one who looked so lost, so dazed, such questions. I was 11 years old, just three and a half months older than David. Mom and Dad were his godparents.

My father, a stern man of sturdy Germanic stock, seemed mystified as to how he'd suddenly become the father of a black child; somehow, something seemed out of whack with us. And David, ebony-skinned David, stood out like a film negative of the rest of us.

I hated him. Not at first — I mean, we were great friends when we were just friends, but it was different when he was my brother, got all that doting and attention from my parents; they were trying to engineer a comfortable readjustment and give him space to mourn. David didn't seem to recognize that the crash had really happened, that his parents were really dead. And in the midst of that haze of denial, my parents suddenly didn't seem to have time to give me any attention.

The Bickner kids were a grubby, scrappy pair of boys training to follow in their father's white trash footsteps. Their future was to become two more on the town's long list of habitual offenders, bump from job to shitty job, land in the county jail occasionally. They lived only a few blocks away, up Argent Way, which crossed Hughes near our house. Johnny, held back in 8th grade, and Joey, who like David and I was about to begin sixth grade, already pedaled, sullen and sunken-eyed, around the neighborhood, trying to look like bikers, toughs, bullies. Unlit cigarettes poached from their father's pack dangled from their lips. They used to find sticks, fallen branches, and clang them along the wrought-iron bars of Auntie Agnes' fence, taunting Fritz into a hulking, snarling rage. I told you that Fritz loved us neighbor kids. Really, Fritz loved every kid in the neighborhood except for the Bickners, and the Bickners worked to earn that dog's wrath.

David was the first black person in our neighborhood. There was a kid named Cullen, who was not white, but not black either, and none of us actually knew how to peg his pedigree. And we didn't dare ask, either, for fear of showing our stupidity. Cullen had black hair in great, wavy curls atop his bronze head. His quick, confident smile, his humor and good looks, charmed us all.

Cullen welcomed David aboard on our missions to Exchange Park to climb the things we weren't supposed to climb. I felt betrayed. I fumed in silence when Cullen, too, suddenly divided his attention between us. To me, my unexpected brother was stealing away my parents and my friends.

We climbed up the outside of the rocket-shaped platform and slide, scrambled backwards up the slide. From the outside, we wedged our feet through the bars meant to keep kids in, following the curving steps all the way to the top, 30 feet up. Simple! I remember watching from inside, as David edged along the rocket's outer bars, unaware in that child's way of the danger he was putting himself in. As his bronze hands clutched the bars before me, and he braced to climb higher, I thought: How easy it would be to give his fingers a quick punch and watch him fall; it would be a terrible accident, and my parents would rush in to comfort me over the loss of my best friend, my new brother.

I didn't do it. I wasn't quick enough, and the moment passed, and in the aftermath, as my brother scaled the rocket, my heart clutched and lungs ached like I'd been kicked by a horse. My eyes burned with guilty, salty tears. I had seriously considered killing David when he had done absolutely nothing to me, apart from survive his parents' deaths. I never told anyone about that.

We'd all scrape our nickels and dimes together to buy ourselves a bottle of grape Nehi, a kid's candy-sweet soda. Whenever any of us felt the need, we'd find the bottle sitting there, on a picnic table near the slide, and take a pull from the shared treat.

Sometimes the Dewitt boys would come along. The chain-link barrier around the top of the public picnic shelter inspired us. The warning, the very *verboten*ness it implied, was too much to resist. It set us to work thinking up ways to conquer the barrier and get up onto the roof. Here's how we did it: The fencing ran along the top of the shelter's flat roof. We climbed, following it along the edge and around the corner, to where it ended — apparently at the point Parks officials determined too ambitious a goal for troublemaking kids. The shelter always seemed to be littered with empty Old Style quart bottles in the mornings, before the clean-up crews came through.

Beyond the park, just to the West, flanked by Conger Street to the north and the Cedar River to the south, stood an old Army outpost, long disused. But gravel pits with obstacle-course tires remained, as did the boarded-up beige-brick building we could never seem to find a way into. And the best basic-training hazard of all: The manhole-covered tubes the Army had left accessible. The steel manhole covers were heavy for kids our age, but swung up on their hinges with sufficient effort and determination. They were about eight feet deep and dank, moss clinging to pocks in the poured cement. Rounded, tread-textured iron rungs embedded in the concrete served as steps. They were treacherously slick when it rained.

Life in working-class Waterloo was a relentless saturation campaign, a marinade of attitudes suspicious of education, pointlessly aggressive, a *walk tough don't act too smart* zeitgest that knocked people down and kept them there. It was something that the population, somehow, had gotten convinced to perpetuate. We'd see a kid as optimistic as the rest of us at the end of the school year come back from summer sullen, reeking of cigarette smoke, picking fights — a kid who'd given up and decided to go nowhere. A kid beaten by Waterloo. We'd watched it happen to the Bickners' older brother, Jerry. He took up his father's brand of cigarettes and anger, found a shitty-wage job at the DX, and dropped out of high school. Then Waterloo took Johnny, then Joey.

But we were at the park, we Waterloo kids still too young to have had our dreams beaten out of us by the constant pressure of that attitude. Even Janet, one of only two girls our age around, had snuck down to the park with us.

When I came scraping down the too-dry slide, I found Cullen there, talking with her. Janet motioned me over with a nod that flipped aside the short, straight, raven hair her half-Japanese ancestry had bestowed upon her. "Come on," Cullen said with that smile. So I did. They led David and I across the park, past giant concrete cylinders mounted on their sides for kids to scamper through, over to the old Army grounds. Between the two of us, Cullen and I were able to lift the lid on one. Janet descended, then me, then Cullen. But David wasn't so sure.

"This place doesn't look safe," he said, a wave of his hand taking in the entire compound. And he was right — it really wasn't.

"Jeez, David, no one'll know," Cullen said. His words did not convince my new brother. Cullen stretched out his hand, offering the bottle of Nehi.

"David," I said, the fog of shame making me feel more brotherly toward him, "trust me. It's OK."

David met my green eyes with his deep, walnut-brown gaze. And he did — he did trust me. After all that. Reluctantly, he nodded. He scrambled down the ladder after us.

"What's all this?" I said.

Cullen smiled serenely. "Janet says she'll show us if we show ours."

Janet grinned, her back straight as a bolt, her chin jutting, defiant.

And so we did. Don't ever let anyone convince you that children are free of sexuality, that they are innocent. We were not. None of us would ever have let on what I'd done with Cullen there, or he with me, or that Janet had chosen to experiment with David. I doubt I even could have said the word *fuck* at that age — or known exactly what the word meant. Our parents would have had some godawful punishment for us, their sexually naïve, not-yet-oriented, interracially experimental, anything goes children, if they'd found out. They would have rounded us up to make sure we all knew none of us was to see the others again, not even in school. I'm not even sure you could call it *fucking*. It wasn't — not really. I think I'd have to say that it was more a negotiation, kids trying to figure out what it was all about, how, exactly, it all worked.

But summer was in its final days, and the city, in its wisdom, had drawn up a new map. To thoroughly integrate the schools, they said. Like a gerrymandered Texas voting map, a single line snaked up the hill along Argent and snatched away David and I, leaving Janet and Cullen in our old school, Lincoln, just down the hill. They could walk to school, but we'd be riding in one of the dungy school buses across town. The Bickners already went to Roosevelt — expelled, we knew, from Lincoln last year. Roosevelt would be our new destination.

The neighborhood parents were not happy. Roosevelt was a black school, part of the chain of schools that emptied into East High. Because all of the white families, including those of Waterloo's petty local politicians, sent their kids to West High, the black schools were severely underfunded. My Mom and Dad openly talked of East High as a firetrap. That was where they'd gone, and that was why they'd decided to keep the house on Hughes, rather than sell off her part of the estate: to keep me in the West High line of school succession. Now that plan was ruined. Death ran young in Mom's family. Everything seemed to. The house belonged partly to my mother, but my grandparents had left it jointly to both her and her brother, Karl, who wasn't in any hurry to get the money.

I don't know why I went back to the park alone; maybe I was just bored — none of the other kids seemed to be out and about. David was home, playing with what were now *our* toys in what was now *our* shared bedroom. Maybe I just wanted to go and play without him around. Maybe because it had just rained a cold, hard downpour, and playing with our toys inside was getting old. But anyway, I did, I walked all the way down the hill to Exchange Park and, bored, decided to climb the picnic shelter alone. My usual handholds in the chainlink were slick and cold enough from the rain that my knuckles got sore, my fingers quickly numb. The chainlink along the flat, tarred rooftop was about 12 feet up. When my lead foot slipped on the slick, narrow edge of the roof, my stomach curdled. I had no easy way down. Cold, wet blacktop ran alongside the shelter. My second foot slipped before I could replant the first, and I hung there from the chainlink and for a second it seemed like I could just hold on, just hang there, like maybe I didn't have to fall. But my weight was too much for my cold, sore fingers. The fence bowed outward, dangling me away from the building, rusty snags biting into my fingers, and I just could not hold on.

I fell. My stomach squeezed in on itself. I didn't know what would happen. I've since heard people describe this moment as though it were flight, but I wasn't flying, I was a rock, a chunk of asphalt plunging toward a hard, paved surface. I must have jammed out my left arm to cushion the blow, because it met the unyielding blacktop with an agonizing crunch. The rest of me crashed down on it. I don't remember much about the walk back to the house on Hughes, except that it was a slow, cautious process; if I twisted my body too much as I walked, the pain whited my vision over like a lens flare, and I had to stop, catch my breath, and squint back the tears. If I breathed too deeply, that hurt like hell too.

None of us were allowed to go to the park unsupervised again. My folks made calls to the other parents. My fractured ulna earned me a cast and sling and a scathing indictment of how expensive my irresponsibility had been.

The last night before the new school year, the sun was still high up in the late-August sky at dinnertime, still, unforgivably, shining bright with invitation. This was what was merciless about summer ending so soon: Why wouldn't the sunset get in line with the school schedule? David and I decided we would head out into the neighborhood after the meal and see who was around while we still could. It was a school night, so we had to be back early, way before sunset. David finished up ahead of me. I told him I'd catch up. I felt like I was around him all the time anyway; it was annoying. So he headed out ahead of me. This was Hughes, our neighborhood — we were safe.

Outside I heard Fritz bellowing savage oaths of wrath at something, could see him leaping up against the black wrought-iron barrier that bordered his yard.

I stepped out the front door, looking to see what was aggravating the huge dog. Half a block away I saw Joey Bickner holding David's arms, clamping them from behind, as Johnny, the unlit smoke jumping around in his lips, pounded his finger into David's chest, yelling. Johnny held an empty grape Nehi bottle by its neck. He swung it down against the concrete abutment of Agnes' raised terrace. He must have seen that in a movie, thought it was cool. Fritz snarled. He lunged with everything he had, bashing his face into the iron fencing, a teddy bear turned raging beast. And incredibly, I remember thinking, *Broken glass? Kids play around here.*

Johnny waved the sharp, jagged edge of the bottle's shattered bottom at David's face, the dirty, straw-like burr of Bickner-family hair spraying out at all angles.

Johnny was sneering, dominant. The only word I could make out from him this far away was *nigger.* David was the negative again, no matter what. The bigger boy buried a fist in David's stomach; David tried to double over, but Joey pulled him back to his feet.

"Bickner!" I said. "Get away from him!" I grabbed my bat from the yard and ran toward them. Johnny Bickner knew it would take me a few seconds to reach them and decided to get in another cheap shot before I could close the distance. He dropped what was left of the bottle, cocked a fist back and pounded it across David's eye, then went after his arm, punching again and again until I was almost close enough to club them. Joey let go and David sagged, shuddering, the left eye already swelling. I swung the bat with my right arm, forcing the Bickners back.

"Whatsamatter faggot?" Johnny said, sneering. "Don't like yer girlfriend doin' niggers?"

The bottom dropped out of my stomach. *Niggers?* I thought. *Faggot?* I felt heat radiating from my face as it flushed with angry, humiliated red. How could they possibly know about Janet and David? We hadn't told anyone. I swung the bat again, a wild, one-armed swing, but they were a dozen feet away, laughing. I never could hit anything with that bat.

"Maybe your mamma does black guys," said Joey. "Yeah — how else do you get a black brother? Maybe that's whatcher so pissed off about!"

I stepped menacingly forward, aiming the bat for Joey's square-headed temple. Way down Argent, I saw Garland Bickner lope unsteadily onto one of the brown, dead crabgrass islands that dotted the Bickners' cracked, dirty front yard. The man wore only blue jeans, no shirt or socks, and low enough they might not even have been buttoned. His beer belly swung liquidly, bulbously before him. He leaned unsteadily on the tireless rusted Chevy he had up on blocks. I could see that dirty gray, strawlike mess of hair atop his head even from that far.

"Goddamn you little bastards, you get the fuck down here an' eat!" he said.

Johnny and Joey Bickner snapped to an upright, military-like posture and blanched white, their faces suddenly bloodless. Silent tears and sudden worry flushed across their faces. Their eyes flitted nervously at one another for a moment, then they broke into an all-out run, barreling with everything they had toward home. Garland Bickner had risen for the day, and he had spoken.

I reached down to help David to his feet, but he flinched away in pain; my right hand had squeezed his left, where the Bickner boys had landed so many punches.

I walked to his other side, slipped my right arm under his, and pulled his heaving form to its feet. Fritz barked after the Bickner boys from within the wrought-iron border of his domain.

David fixed his dark-eyed gaze on me, his expression full of *Why?*.

I didn't know.

"Come on," I said, "let's go home."

When the first Monday of school came, my mother loaded us down with Six Million Dollar Man lunchboxes — the kind that got us laughed at by the older kids — and tote bags full of school supplies, and walked us to the front door to see us off to the bus stop. "Don't go getting yourselves in any trouble," my father said. "And don't ruin your new clothes."

The first day of classes at Roosevelt Middle School, I did not even manage to make it into the building before I went against his wishes. A horde of black kids saw David and me coming and intercepted us before we could reach the front door. I'd never seen so many, and not another white kid in sight.

The ringleader, kind of a short kid with an immense, malicious smile stabbed a finger into my chest. "Where you goin', White Boy?" he said. *White Boy*. He was using it as a name for me, an insult.

I was terrified. I knew black people — well, some black people, David and his family. People always said things about them, always said they were violent, dangerous, criminal; West High kids knew not to walk around near East High. But none of that was true — I knew people like David and had known his parents. That was all garbage, stereotypes, stuff for racists.

I glanced at David, whose eyes stared back, unblinking. This was altogether new for him, too. There were about 15 kids gathered around us, laughing, jeering, but only at me — not David. It was the first time in my life I'd ever seen more black kids in one place than white.

"I said," he said, "where you goin', honky?"

Honky? I thought. I'd never been the target of a racial slur before.

The ringleader, though, was cocky, and my paralysis only made him braver. He swung a fist out, thumping it into my arm — the left one. The scene disappeared under a crushing, searing wave, my eyesight whited out by the pain of the attack on my broken, useless arm. I fell, ripping my pants and skinning my knee on the concrete. I knew how angry my parents would be at the economic assault on my new school clothes. There was a numbing strike on my mouth.

When I opened my eyes again and looked up, the ringleader was looking David up and down, pacing back and forth. He could not seem to decide what to do about a black kid he'd never seen before going around with a white kid. He couldn't seem to find a way to make sense of the two of us, together. The ringleader — whose name, I later learned, was Darnell Redd — pointed a finger at David and asked, "Fuck you doin' with White Boy, boy?"

But his tone was half-hearted. With David too stunned to reply, Darnell Redd was losing interest. "Come on, y'all," he said to the deafening, obnoxious group of black kids. He led them, his chest puffed out in triumph, to the playground. So that was me: the white kid. White Boy. I was the one who didn't belong.

I thought for a second that no one in our neighborhood had called David "Black Boy," but then I remembered the Bickners and what they had called him.

David was at my side. "Come on," he said. "Come on, get up now." He was careful to pull me up by my right arm, avoiding all contact with the left. "Got to be a nurse's office here. Come on."

The arm was fine. It ached like hell, but Darnell Redd hadn't managed to do more damage. My lip was swollen, numb, torn against my teeth. When David and I walked past the principal's office on my way back to class, there sat Darnell Redd, a broad grin on his face as he awaited whatever impotent punishments the principal, Mrs. Jayden, might visit upon him.

As I looked in on the smug, defiant bully, it seemed to let itself out of my mouth, form of its own volition. Under my breath, I heard myself say it.

David stopped. His posture stiffened. And immediately, I wanted not to have said it, not to have thought it. I would have done anything to un-say it. But it was too late. I had betrayed him — betrayed my younger brother. I thought I saw him shudder, but he turned away from me and hurried down the dark hall.

Other students talked to me, some of the school's meager Caucasian population. They all seemed to slink along, stealthy kids trying not to attract attention.

"Darnell's father's in and out of jail all the time," said Danny Sparks, a slight kid with dirty blonde hair and a posture that said he was ready for a fistfight. "Darnell isn't afraid of anything on earth but that man. Principal Jayden knows it, but she can't seem to think up with a punishment that makes any difference."

"Why don't they just kick him out?" I said.

"I dunno," said Dan Sparks. "Maybe they want to give him a chance not to turn into his dad."

I nodded. I was beginning to understand. "This place does that to people, doesn't it?" I said. "But Darnell doesn't seem to care. Maybe he wants to turn into his dad."

Danny Sparks shrugged, looking me over uneasily.

"Look, why you hanging around with a black kid?" he said.

"He's — " I said. I hesitated, not knowing why. The words just felt out of place, somehow. "He's my brother," I said, finally. But I knew what he meant — the message at Roosevelt was loud and clear. Danny Sparks gave me another doubtful looking over. Then he shrugged, turned, and slunk silently away.

At lunch, David and I sat together, of course. Why wouldn't we? But we sat alone. White kids sat in all-white groups in the gym-turned-lunchroom, the black kids likewise self-segregating at other tables. We ate our bologna-on-Wonderbread sandwiches, then went out to see the playground. It was dismal. The school's brick walls were filthy with accumulated pollution, the paved concrete schoolyard a cataclysm of faults and fissures. We made newcomer mistakes. We kept tripping as we walked, our shoes jamming into pavement raised at the cracks. Our occasional stumbles brought knowing, mocking glances from veteran students. The playground was stocked with decades-old, tarnished jungle gyms and twirlbars worn to a discolored gleam by generations of black girls, spinning end over end on them, one knee locked over the bar, as a dozen such girls did now.

As we walked along, a girl, a tall, coffee-and-cream-complected mulatto, flashed a dazzling smile at me. I walked into David, not watching where I was going, not watching anything except for the girl, her gleaming, long, black braids, her skin darker, richer than my boring, pallid vanilla, but not as dark as David's. I smiled back, my fat lip a stretched, red bubble above my teeth. She was beautiful.

"That's Trisha," he said sullenly, the first words from his mouth since I'd said it. "She's in my first class."

I nodded. There was a sort of man-made cove along this side of the school building, a brick and concrete inlet, an alleyway with training wheels. There, in the shadows cast by the bleak, dirty school building, stood Johnny and Joey Bickner, Johnny now a year older and much bigger than any of the other kids. Couldn't they have done something with him that didn't guarantee that a school bully wouldn't also be the biggest kid around? They eyed David and I as we walked, secretively, but not too secretly, exchanging comments. They wanted us to see their disapproval.

We rounded the corner of the playground to an expanse of chainlink and shattered concrete, more a battleground than a place for children to play. Weeds grew, unchecked, from the larger fissures further out. And I heard David sob. He couldn't hold it back anymore.

I wanted to say something to remove that word, get it out from between us. Un-say it.

"Why'd you say it?" he said.

I saw him through tear-blurred vision; the sky overhead had gone an overcast watercolor grey.

I wanted to say, "That was Waterloo talking." I wanted to say, "I'm sorry, David — I'm so sorry." But I couldn't. Shame cemented me in place, bound my tongue up in a regret I just couldn't find words for.

David forced himself to look at me, forced his eyes to meet mine, and with a fallen look he said, "David?"

And I saw us, finally, for what we were: reflections. Reciprocals. Negatives of one another — David black, surrounded by white, and me, white, surrounded by black.

And I knew what he must be thinking; I knew that he must be rethinking my position among the people we knew, relocating me in his mind alongside Johnny Bickner and Darnell Redd, whose view of people and their place in the world was so black and white it could find no room for the in-between hues of Cullen, or Trisha, even huge old Fritz's rampant shades and tones.

I wanted to squeeze his arm then, like I thought a big brother should. I wanted to tell him, "No more. I promise. It's all right now. It's OK. I'll never say it again. I promise. You're my brother." I wanted to. I really did.

I wish
I had.

Signal to Noise
Excerpted from the novel of the same title.

Disk 1, Side A — Promo Track:

Transmission | Reception

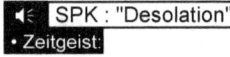

Fall, just past the mid-80s — the heart of the Reagan-Bush reign and the peak of the alt/indie/punk scene in Iowa City.

Every chord, every note, every single guitar strike detonated like the idle-chug of an 18-wheeler. Connor Hegarty never figured out how they made that sound: Exactly like an engine.

Meat Grinder was playing Gabe's Oasis. Connor was coming off a shift DJing at KRUI, his psyche a conflicted mess of high from being on the air and pained by the call from home. He heard their distortion-heavy aural assault building long before he could see the stage, a sonic meltdown the likes of which he had never experienced; mechanical demolition fused with radio noise and a clanging junkyard chorus of found metallic objects repurposed for percussion; a tricked-out bass that showed the scars of by-hand modification, all steel cables and mysterious knobs, glinting additions and switches; two drum kits; and a 55-gallon steel barrel, "MEAT GRINDER," and the band's logo — a pair of meat cleavers crossed in an X — spray-stenciled on. The twin drum kits were a haphazard jumble of shining steel and stands resembling a pair of oil refineries under assault by kong-sized monsters wielding a tree in each hand.

Connor, a sophomore at Iowa, made his way cautiously forward. He'd spent the past few months getting to know the alternative-music scene from the power-pop/indie rock end of things, but had no idea anything like this was going on. He'd never stumbled across such anti-music before.

Once he cleared the curving stairwell's first landing, once he'd worked his way past the doorman at the second landing, once he'd made the entrance to the upper bar, which housed the stage and the stacks, the band came into view.

Towering over six feet tall, her hair a halogen explosion, skin an alabaster tint that rendered her features in high contrast, glow and shadow and little else, the grrl savaged a towering bank of home-fabricated noise boxes. Somehow the most magnetic presence in a stage littered with effects pedals, miked sawhorses, hazardous-looking creations of steel, the other musicians. A severe, dangerous beauty about her, broad cheekbones and a high forehead swept with that hair.

Connor watched, trying to make sense of her.

Meat Grinder had hung jagged sheets of plexiglass on hooks and chains from the aging iron girders that ran across the ceiling of the club, each around five by five feet, each bearing some spattered and slashed image done up in red and black. In the reflective surface of a panel bearing the image of a sinewy forearm and hand clutching a hunting knife, he caught just a hint of metal cabling flexing among the muscles, under the skin covering her arm, the tattooed barbed-wire ringing her biceps stabbing outward, made real, somehow. Audio and electrical wiring and cabling emerged from the flesh of her hands and forearms, snaking into the rear of her noise-making set-up.

She turned, casting a look over her shoulder, out over the seething mass before the stage. Brilliant twin spotlights slashed forth from her eyes like a set of high-beams, carving twin swaths through the club's thick, smoggy atmosphere — coming to rest on him.

And in the wash of that sonic tide, bathed in the penetrating light of her high-beam gaze, Connor's moment crystallized, time flowing only between the two of them, all else grinding to a halt.

Connor felt altered, transmogrified. He raised his own arm before him, arching his wrist and splaying the fingers wide. He saw a seething hybrid of cable and muscle, metal and meat flexing just beneath a translucent latex-like skin, its surface covered in some sort of clotted, ruddy-brown gore. What *was* she? What was she doing to him?

Her caustic, high-beam gaze soaked him, boiling away the external and revealing a vision of things lurking within.

The brilliance of her stare pounding down on him —

Held. Connor. Hegarty. Mesmerized.

Connor could only gape at the magnificent chrome-like grille of teeth glimpsed through lips parted by her snarl.

His novice sense of alt-rock cool still had its training wheels, and she scared the affectation cool straight the hell out of him. Like a cobra holding a sparrow paralyzed in its gaze. How had she even spotted him through all that?

The vision faded, spectral. She returned her gaze to the task at hand, cables no longer seeming to erupt straight from her own flesh.

He ran his hands back through his newly blue alt-music hair experiment. That menacing punk-rock bad girl's leather and dramatic make-up look was like a dare, bondage and badass — it said: *Fuck me at your peril*. He'd never laid eyes on anything like the hardcore Amazon on stage before him. She wore gleaming pants of some synthetic black material, a heavy-link chain looped twice around her waist, and a smeared white t-shirt emblazoned with a skull-and-test-pattern logo and the words "Psychic TV," the sleeves cut roughly away. Connor glimpsed the pocked, tarnished surface of a silvery pendant — a slash-script A bursting the bounds of a circle, the symbol for *anarchy* — swinging, pendulous, from a leather cord strung around her neck.

Connor had spotted some Psychic TV LPs as he flipped through the bins at the Record Collector earlier, trying to judge an album by its cover. But the name didn't communicate anything to him, so he'd put the records back. What the hell was a Psychic TV?

His black t-shirt said "Sonic Youth" in hand-spattered bleach text that had yielded a corroded white to orange effect. He wore torn army-surplus pants, and black Converse high tops.

The doorman sat at a card table, his stringy off-brown hair held in place by a Peterbilt cap and falling just below his shoulders. He shook faintly, happily.

"Who's that?" Connor yelled at the doorman, pointing toward the stage. His voice strained to cut through the din.

"Meat Grinder!"

"No, man — *her!*"

"That's The Siren, dude!" he said, his face all nodding, tweaking, sweating grin and saucer-sized pupils. "Watch out!"

Connor thought the tweaker meant that The Siren was dangerous in her own punk-rock right. Then the doorman added: "She's totally married to that big guitar guy! Real-life husband-wife hardcore team!"

Connor stared at the two. The guitarist was shorter than The Siren, and heavy-set, around 250, a hunched white guy with shoulder-length dirty-blonde dreads swinging, obscuring his face and head. Faded sweatshirt torn down to a T, faded tattoos coiling down tensed arms. The dreadlocked man looked to be around 30, though it was difficult to tell through the dreads and facial hair. The Siren looked closer to Connor's age than the guitarist's. The union did not seem feasible to him: A noise-sculpting goddess wed to a guitar-wielding troll?

The Siren stood onstage, middle-left, at a bank of orphic, unidentified equipment, a rack of electronics and machinery towering over her, metallic synths spliced and soldered together from kits and bolted into metal boxes, wires trailing from behind, coaxial tentacles entwining them. With a confident, bowlike arch to her back, The Siren faced rear-right, mostly away from the audience.

Connor carved out a spot in a crowd of dark, otherworldly anthropoid forms at the edge of the pit to take in the scene. He'd been to indie shows before and was passingly familiar with the crowd that turned up for those, but he didn't know these people. The air was a hazy cocktail of cigarette smoke, engine exhaust, spilled beer, and human sweat. The guitarist, anchored on the left, his strumming hand armored in a chainmail-and-leather glove, some kind of steel picks spot-welded to the fingers. Connor caught the flat-wet white of eyes rolled back into the guitarist's skull momentarily before the orbs submerged beneath the dreadlock current.

At the stage's fore-right, a spindly male with dark hair short on the sides, a bobbing, sweaty clump of curls spilling down over his eyes. With both hands, he swung a jagged seven-foot mutilation of steel with what looked to Connor like the handle from a saw bolted onto one end; he hauled the strip into position behind him, braced himself, and heaved it in an arc over his head, bringing the far side crashing down onto one of the sawhorses. Faint scars and scrapes punctuated the undersides of his forearms, shirt missing its sleeves and any remnant of a collar, all spraypaint and stains. Connor stopped breathing when he got it: The guy was keeping rhythm with that tear of metal.

Two drummers were obscured from view by the scrapyard on stage and the oily smog in the air, left to right, in the rear. The bass player's features struck a hybrid chord, Far East Asian and African; his hair, a tangle of sculpted, seemingly independent influences, sprayed out in a dozen directions; all-American. Rear-right. They actually had a motor on-stage to rev up, its accelerator pedal alongside the litter of effects pedals and banks.

And the striking, postmod, post-Amazon performing in a cabal of damaged freaks, savagely graceful, consummate in her element.

The sound was utterly, utterly unique. Connor didn't even have a name for what he was hearing. It involved more metal than he'd ever seen any band use, but the music was not *metal*; *metal* as a rubric for a type of music was already taken by the bad-home-perm high-school dropouts who drank quarts of cheap all-American macrobrew in plain brown bags in city parks after hours (to show everyone they were *breakin' the law, breakin' the law!*). The guys whose favorite songs always seem to find their way back to partying, or finding some way to escape from the streets of this blue-collar/one-horse/workin' class town where the only thing to do is cruise the strip and pick fights with other people couldn't get away.

Meat Grinder were not just making noise; Connor had an unhampered understanding of that much. They were clearly performing specific pieces — specific songs — riffing off each other, bobbing and weaving, driving through the noise, carving movement from dissonance.

The songs never actually stopped: The coherence of one movement would begin to break down, melt slowly into chaos, its solidity flowing into cacophony; Meat Grinder would wallow in the din, harvesting audio from bad-reception AM and feedback, creating, blazing, collapsing pathways through the noise; then, in time, a new piece would begin to organize, begin to build itself into coherence. Into order. The music these lunatics were making was, he began to realize, four-dimensional; parts arose from the tumult on the left and dove to the middle, dancing right, and back, or bursting suddenly in the middle, somehow shifting from rear to front, the volume of individual pieces of sound fading in, rising, falling, all churning forward through time: a slithering, sinewy juggernaut.

The band didn't even look at the audience.

A swell in the human tide dragged Connor into the current of the pit, an arena of organized riot: Punk kids and braless, tough-ass grrls threw themselves into bruising collisions, stopping immediately to pull any fallen comrade from the floor, then back to the punishment of the slam. In the pit, all were in it together, every mosher for and against every other. A release of stress and violence, a collectively controlled form of anarchy — a way to get it all the fuck out of your system.

The pit, throbbing with blood-red light from the stage, became a hot, drifting bank of greasy steam, individual spotlights cleaving through the smog.

Connor rode the violence for a minute, then edged his way out.

A sweat-covered hardcore fan, fingers of hair taped in the way that precedes dreadlocks, fought his way out of the pit, a scrunch of disembodied anger for a face, his Shadowy Men On A Shadowy Planet t-shirt and army-surplus pants splotched with sweat and scuff from the floor. Caught by the human tide, he washed up next to Connor.

Ever hear Meat Grinder up close before, man?! he demanded. Meat Grinder was blasting so hard the guy needed subtitles.

Connor shook his head *no*; this was a new experience. But he'd heard some noise he could compare it to.

Earlier, sitting in the production studio at KRUI with goth-show host Ashe, Connor had tried to listen to tracks from Skinny Puppy's "Mind: The Perpetual Intercourse" and an LP by SPK called "Leichenshrei." He hadn't been prepared for that level of intensity. He'd had to get away. But now, listening to Meat Grinder, he was beginning to get it.

Meat Grinder's set wound down and band members began to leave the stage, digital delays and reverb rioting across the club, the pounding tides of sound crashing along. It began with The Siren, who disappeared completely when the red spotlight on her was extinguished. The guitarist hanging his guitar, strings facing inward, on the custom grating of his amp; the bass player following suit; the others stepping back, disengaging from their gear, and departing, the waves continuing the show on auto-pilot. The vision of her had swept aside the lingering anger he'd felt from the phone call, her tides of audio sculpture washing it away.

Connor checked his watch; he worked his way through the crowd, back to the doorman, and asked him when the next group was coming on — some local freakshow called Stickdog; he'd only read the name on concert fliers.

"'Bout 20 minutes," he said. "They're somethin', huh? Meat Grinder?"

Connor nodded, distantly. He couldn't get The Siren's paralyzing high-beam gaze out of his mind, the waves of the noise in which she swam crashing over him — feedback — reverb — distortion — he'd found something completely, intoxicatingly unique.

"What — " Connor said, stammering a little, "What the fuck kind of music is that, my man?"

The doorman grinned ear-to-ear in his giddy reply with the term Connor was missing: "Industrial!"

◀ *... kuff-k-skffksss... kuff-k-skffksss... kuffsss ...* *[End Promo track]*

Writing the Review

"Writing the Review" first appeared in the journal Pank, Issue 4, January 2010.

5.1   What do I write, for fuck's sake? What do I write? And who do I write it to?

0.1   Skyler. Fans of underground hardcore know him as a genius. The police know him as a repeat offender of certain minor laws, never a felony, always misdemeanor offences — public intox, disturbing the peace, third-party suspicion of domestic violence in their home, possession of small amounts of marijuana ...

I know him as a friend.

The first time I saw him was at a concert by a groundbreaking, fuck-off attitude hardcore band called Meat Grinder. He seemed possessed — a towering figure wracked in the thralls of some sort of creation fervor, eyes rolled back in his head as he worked over his guitar, facing his amp, feeding back, reworking the feedback into the main arc of the music, his stringy hair waving before his face, stuck with sweat to his forehead. His instrument was screaming out first a melody then, with a digital delay repeating the part, he was adding layers to the song, becoming its lead and second guitarists, its architect, its creator.

I write about music for a magazine that covers all of the underground stuff — live music, hardcore, punk, industrial — you name it. Well, almost; we steer clear of any form of country, even alt-country or that y'all-ternative stuff that's been coming out of Austin. Hearing Skyler play for the first time could change your religion.

0.x   ~~Skyler.~~ Kyrinne. Fans of underground hardcore know ~~him~~ her as a genius's babe. ~~The police know him as a repeat offender of certain minor laws, never a felony, always misdemeanor offences — public intox, disturbing the peace, third-party suspicion of domestic violence in their home, possession of small amounts of marijuana ...~~ There's no secret that she and Skyler are together; but with her high-arching halogen blond hair, buzzed down on the left side, grown long everywhere else, with her stunning, rock-star stature and beauty, the fans also know that she is *verboten*. At what penalty, they don't ask — they simply don't even try to go there. They admire Skyler's work with sound, and they envy him for having Kyrinne. She plays a smaller role in the band. She plays the steady bassline that anchors Skyler. He tells me, sometimes, how bad he needs that. He quotes Charlie Parker, the jazz musician, to me. "He was playing in Dan Wall's Chili House, a Harlem jazz club back in 1939, when he had this moment, right? Once Parker figured out that he could do anything — fucking *anything*, man — as long as he could resolve it back to the main theme of the song in time, his head broke open.

Talking about it, Parker said, 'I came alive. I could fly.' When I have the guitar in my hands, I know how he felt when he said it."

0.4   Skyler. Fans of underground hardcore know him as a genius. ~~The police know him as a repeat offender of certain minor laws, never a felony, always misdemeanor offences — public intox, disturbing the peace, third-party suspicion of domestic violence in their home, possession of small amounts of marijuana ...~~ But I know the real Skyler, the real deal.

Skyler's first love was heroin. A close second was his guitar. Kyrinne came in a distant third. On the outside, in public she didn't seem to mind. But I started coming to all their shows, I started hanging with them after hours, and I started to see through the public veneer; I got to know Skyler; I got to know the real deal.

2.1   Kyrinne is glowing, a savage beauty, as Skyler sits soundlessy in their living room, guitar in hands. He is lost in the song, his eyes rheumy, unfocussed. The drummer and vocalist are transient characters who won't last six months with these two, but for now, they're part of the most innovative hardcore act in town. The opening band, Deaf Lepers, have come along; a solution of coke cleverly packaged in a sinus-spray bottle is making the rounds, as is a pot pipe.

7.1   I want to take her for a night out. I want to walk with her —

"Read your write-up," he says. It is past 3 am, the band are beat from playing, but way too pumped up to call it a night.

"My write-up?"

"Pigface, man." He lowers his voice to sound like a TV news anchor. "'Every madman industrialist's twisted nightmare dream just came true, and it calls itself Pigface,'" he says. Your word carries weight. Street weight, anyway — not major-label weight. When you gonna write us up?"

"How about now? That was a hell of a show, Skyler," I say. I decline the pipe — the stuff only makes me sleep, and fast. I'm waiting for the nasal-spray bottle.

"Right now?" he says. "Here?"

I stretch. "No. In the morning. I need to get some rest and get the ringing out of my head before I can write."

He sighs, bored but impatient at this loss of immediate gratification.

"First thing, Skyler," I say, "relax."

5.2   What do I write for fuck's sake? What do I write? And who do I write it to?

2.2   "Kyrinne," he says, but he can't be bothered to finish the sentence. He tosses her the keys; I need a lift home.

0.5   Skyler. Fans of underground hardcore know him as a genius. ~~The police know him as a repeat offender of certain minor laws, never a felony, always misdemeanor offences — public intox, disturbing the peace, third-party suspicion of domestic violence in their home, possession of small amounts of marijuana ...~~ But I know the ~~real Skyler, the real deal.~~ idiot savant.

     It didn't take me long to figure out, once I was tight with the band. When the guitar is in his grip, he explodes with genius, an artist in his own element. Other times, though, he can't be bothered with the rest of the world. I asked him once why he didn't spread his wings a little, try writing some with one of those programs or some electronic equipment. He huffed a laugh, dismissive, turned his head, and waved a lazy wave. When my review of their album hits the streets, I find him at a booth in the Deadwood, a refugee seeking asylum from the daylight.

     "I read your write-up, man," he says. He picks up the magazine and intones with just enough of a mockering edge to shit me, "'Meat Grinder are one way-the-fuck-out-there recording project. Who knows what makes them tick? The single, *Father*, is nothing more, nothing less than five minutes of Skyler's industrial-grade guitar feedback sculpting, am radio noise, and the metronome-steady beat of Kyrinne's bass keeping — and barely keeping — this track in touch with *Terra Firma*. All throughout, though, the guitarist is airborne." He slaps the magazine down on the table. "Shit, man," he says, then dismisses the review with a lazy, backhanded wave.

     Uh-huh, I think, *You can't hold down a job, your kinda-wife works a day job to keep you in guitar strings and smack, and you think you get to critique my writing*. This is what I think, but it is not what I say. If I say this, things might get chilly between us, and I don't want to lose access to him, 'cause if I lose access to him, I lose access to her.

0.6   Skyler. Fans of underground hardcore know him as a genius. ~~The police know him as a repeat offender of certain minor laws, never a felony, always misdemeanor offences — public intox, disturbing the peace, third-party suspicion of domestic violence in their home, possession of small amounts of marijuana ...~~ But I know ~~the real Skyler, the real deal.~~ ~~idiot savant.~~ him as a cuckold.

     ...

2.3   "Kyrinne," he says, but he can't be bothered to finish the sentence. He tosses her the keys; I need a lift home.

In the van, she says, "So. What are you gonna say about the show?"

"My first impressions of Skyler's genius with that guitar," I say. "But he seems distracted, y'know? When he's not playing, it's like he's checked out or something — like he leaves his body behind and ventures off somewhere else."

Kyrinne nods to this, twice.

"What do you think?" I say. "I mean, you anchor him to the song."

"To more than just that," she says. I wait for more, but the moments pass without words. She pulls into a parking spot in front of my building. I'm intrigued about that comment she floated, though. Does she have more insight to share, something that might let me shed some insight on the band's inner workings, Skyler's psychology, anything?

"Come in for a drink?" I say.

She nods — again, two quick, staccato nods.

I've barely got the locks unlatched when I feel her arms enclose me; she's broiling like a star with sudden passion, and we wind up on the floor, fucking, clothes jettisoned in a furious rush.

3.1   As we lie, panting, I feel the rugburn already on my knees, and I say, "More than I'd expected out of a ride home."

"He can't know," she says. "Skyler. If he understood how alone I am, it'd hurt him; if he knew we did this without knowing that, he probably wouldn't even care."

I sit up on an elbow. "It's that bad?" I ask. "You guys are young — too young to have drifted apart."

"We were never all that together, except when we play. Sometimes I'm afraid that if I'm not there to anchor him, he'd never make it back."

"But what do you mean about how alone you are? You're beautiful. He can't be tired of you."

"We've never been like that very much," she says. "It's complicated. He'd never get by without me. I'm his rock, the one thing that keeps him functioning in the real world."

0.4   Skyler. Fans of underground hardcore know him as a genius. ~~The police know him as a repeat offender of certain minor laws, never a felony, always misdemeanor offences — public intox, disturbing the peace, third-party suspicion of domestic violence in their home, possession~~

~~of small amounts of marijuana ...~~ But I know ~~the real Skyler, the real deal. idiot savant.~~ him as a ~~cuckold~~ friend.

Kyrinne and I have been seeing a lot of each other. I don't know how long they've been sexless, but she burns like phosphorous every single time. I wonder how he ever managed to become indifferent to that.

0.41   Skyler. Fans of underground hardcore know him as a genius. ~~The police know him as a repeat offender of certain minor laws, never a felony, always misdemeanor offences — public intox, disturbing the peace, third-party suspicion of domestic violence in their home, possession of small amounts of marijuana ...~~ But I know the ~~real Skyler, the~~ real deal.

Skyler's real name is Wilberfarce, Kyrinne tells me. "Do not ever, ever let him know that you know," she says. *I can see why he upgraded his handle's hip-factor,* I think, but I don't say it. I don't want her to think I'm petty.

Skyler's first love was heroin. A close second was his guitar. Kyrinne came in a distant third. On the outside, in public, she didn't seem to mind. But I started coming to all their shows, I started hanging with them after hours, and I started to see through the public veneer; I got to know Skyler; I got to know the real deal. Skyler needed smack. He'd let himself get addicted — which, with heroin, *really* isn't difficult. So he needs the stuff. And, being his friend, I sometimes buy a dime and bring it by for him.

1.1   *Cuckold.* If I say this, things will get chilly between us fast, and I don't want to lose access to him, 'cause if I lose access to him, I lose access to her. I come by about 7:00 with a gift for my friend Skyler. When I knock, I hear someone come to the door, see the peephole go dark for a second, then light again. Kyrinne opens the door. She holds an ice pack to her right eye. Skyler is left-handed.

"Kyr, what — ?" I start, but she cuts me off, points a finger at me.

"You can't judge him," she says, her voice harsh and quiet. "He's hardly ever like this."

I feel a swell of bravado, though. "Where is he?"

She shrugs. "I was talking with him about maybe getting part-time work. He was playing his guitar, his eyes all fogged over, y'know, and he wasn't paying any attention to me, so I asked, "Hey, are you even in there?"'

I nod. "So suddenly his eyes focus, it's like he's back, he's out of the music, and outta left field, he realizes he's not in the zone anymore, and he's pissed off."

She stops. I wait, but that's all the words she has on the story, so I reach out to hold her. But she pulls back and looks around, wide-eyed. "Not out where everyone can see," she says.

At first I think she's afraid someone will see us in an intimate moment and tell him, but that's not it; she doesn't want to hurt him.

"Doesn't he deserve a little pain?" I say, but she wanders away through their livingroom and into the kitchen, returning with two cold cans of beer, never answering. "Look, is he gonna be gone for a long time?" I ask. "Long enough for us to be alone together?"

She shrugs. "He's unpredictable when he's like this. He could come through the door right now, he might not for a couple of days."

"What about my place?"

She shakes her head. "I'm not going out with a black eye. Someone might see."

Why would that be bad? I think, and I think the expression on my face gives away my exasperation. But I know the answer: She's protecting him, watching over this pseudo-genius so the whole world won't see the broken, barely functional truth. Skyler suddenly seems childlike to me, and I feel like I'm in a competition with him he doesn't even know about — the battle for Kyrinne. Only how can I be in battle if my opponent doesn't know it.

7.2   I want to take her for a night out. I want to walk with her, kiss her, *hold her hand* —

0.8   I think about telling him, but if I do, do I lose her in the process? Does he shrug it off, but outlaw the two of us ever being alone together anyway? I despise and pity him at the same time.

I hear the keys fumbling at the door. But the unlocking takes longer than it should, the air between us and the door filled with clattering, metal clinking against metal; Skyler can't get the key in the hole.

Kyrinne stands, gives me a sad smile, and goes to open the door. Again, my expression must betray my exasperation, but what else can I do? I'm stuck.

She opens the door, and there he is, the guitar genius, his face red and wet; she embraces him and I keep hearing her tell him, "It's okay, baby, it's okay ..."

3.1   When he looks up and sees me, the confusion shows on his face, and I feel like a deer trapped in headlights. Then I remember the heroin in my pocket.

I stand, produce the little baggie, and present it to him. And his tears stop, his face brightens, and he walks to my side to take it, leaving Kyrinne behind at the door.

"A good friend," he says. "I was running low. You're just in time."

I shake his hand, then hers, and make my way out. I can't even say it. I can't even acknowledge that I was there after her, not to give him, my *friend,* the heroin — that was just a prop, and excuse.

0.5   Skyler. Fans of underground hardcore know him as a genius. ~~The police know him as a repeat offender of certain minor laws, never a felony, always misdemeanor offences — public intox, disturbing the peace, third-party suspicion of domestic violence in their home, possession of small amounts of marijuana ...~~ But I know ~~the real Skyler, the real deal.~~ idiot savant. him as a ~~cuckold friend.~~ child, barely functional.

Another Saturday night, another Gabe's gig for The Grinder, and I notice something I've never noticed before. The band has a song called "TotalCore," but on the setlists it's spelled "ToatlaCroe." Another, "Piledriver," is jumbled, as well.

After the set, Kyrinne is radiant, positively thermonuclear. I ask Kyrinne about it.

"Oh," she says, shrugging. Then she lowers her voice to a whisper. "Don't tell anyone — Skyler's dyslexic."

"He's that bad?"

She nods. She has no more words for the subject. She has just glossed over the fact that her partner can barely read. I'm shaking my head in wonder, wondering how much else she shields him from. I reach out and grab her arm, startling her. "Listen," I say. "I think I'm in love with you."

0.x Three. Two. One.

7.3   I want to take her for a night out. I want to walk with her, kiss her, *hold her hand* —

0.x Three. Two. One

7.3   I want to take her for a night out. I want to walk with her, kiss her, hold her hand —
        in public.

0.x Three. Two. One.

5.3   What do I write for fuck's sake? What do I write? And who do I write it to?

0.0   ... idiot savant.

It didn't take me long to figure out, once I was tight with the band. When the guitar is in his grip, he explodes with genius, an artist in his own element. Other times, though, he can't be bothered with the rest of the world. I asked him once why he didn't spread his wings a little, try writing some with one of those programs or some electronic equipment. He huffed a dismissive laugh, turned his head, and waved a lazy wave. Now I knew: He communed with the world through his guitar, and with great expertise and intuition. But only through the guitar. How could he ever work with a song-writing app when he could barely read?

5.4   What do I write, for fuck's sake? What do I write?

3.3   Now she's the one who looks caught in the headlights. She gives me that sad smile and shakes her head, twice, slowly.

1.2   Later, Skyler tosses her the keys to take me home from their place, lost in a delirium of strumming, unplugged. When we get to the van, I feel a dangerous urge flood over me; before we pull out, I pull her to me and kiss her full-on. She pushes against me, shoving me away. "What the fuck are you doing?" she asks. "Are you trying to get caught?"

I consider the question. Maybe I am. Maybe I want this out in the open. "I told you," I said, "I think I'm in love with you."

Shaking her head twice, in sharp, decisive arcs, she says, "Oh hell."

This is not what she'd counted on. She takes me to my building and gives me a perfunctory kiss as I climb out. She stares straight ahead as I go. "No more," she says. "I can't handle this. You're getting reckless."

"No more?" I ask, stunned. I feel like a Clydesdale has just kicked an iron-shoed foot into my sternum. My chest burns like the heart of Chernobyl, all radiation and heat and Eastern-Bloc steel.

"None. You can come to our shows, we all like the press you give us, but no more coming back with us. Okay?" She's radiant, the light and heat coming off her like Hiroshima's second sunrise that fateful day.

"But he smacks you around," I say.

"Not much, and not often," she says. "Look, it's complicated. You'll never understand it, and I have no words to explain it, okay?"

And just like that, it's over, and she's driving away. And my chest is exploding, a mushroom cloud broiling away the damp late-night air ...

6.1   I can't sleep, so I start typing in a review of the show. Kyrinne's hair was like a neon-cabernet explosion tonight. I was hoping to talk her into my apartment, but I think I finally pushed her too far. She'd never consider leaving him, I can see that now. Their orbit is entirely too unique, entirely too tight, entirely too dysfunctional for that to happen. I light a smoke and start searching for new metaphors for the noise sculpture Skyler creates when they play live.

The Grinder aren't much as a studio band, I write. *But catch them live. Seriously, it's like the studios confine their sound too much, remove some vital inertia from their live performances. The album track for a song like "Breaker" sounds confined, even claustrophobic on the album. On stage, it's an act of sonic terrorism, an all-out assault on the audience.*

I pen a line or two about Skyler's genius with his chosen instrument — as though he had a choice in the choosing — but they ring hollow, now; the truth is, he seems pathetic, and he has the woman I want to have. The truth is, that façade of musical genius is starting to grate on me. I write a few lines about Kyrinne's rock-steady performance, but quickly realize that I need to delete references to her beauty and the sexy way she bobs her head to the beat, the way her hair sways with it as she holds the songs together. No point being obviously in love with a taken woman. Certainly no point publishing it for the world to diagnose. I feel more disappointed than wounded; Kyrinne is too beautiful, too unique a creation to waste on a smack-addicted, barely literate child-man. *Wilburfarce,* I think, *for god's sake.* But it's her decision. I find myself hating her for it, but I get, now, that my part in their bizarre relationship was just that: a part in *their* bizarre relationship. And that part has just been written out.

5.4   What do I write, for fuck's sake? What do I write? And who do I write it to?

Dashiell

"Dashiell" first appeared in Gargoyle literary journal, Issue 83, November 2008.

Here is Dashiell, no longer the "Dash" of his college youth when, concerned about sounding effeminate, possibly even queer, he'd shortened it; older, not too old, not ag-*ed*, but old enough to have grown and to have learned a few of life's lessons, young enough, say, to be a compelling, believable, even attractive protagonist, and because no story about life's lessons and about the relationships between fathers and sons could be conveyed convincingly if he were too young — young, as in, *Yo, Dash, your hit from the beer bong, man!* — Dashiell is instead, say, in his mid-thirties. Dashiell wears jeans of a non-trendy brand and cut, demonstrating that passing fads in fashion will not waver his essential core fashion sense, and favors button-up shirts with collars, giving some air of formality, yet calculated, nonetheless, to communicate a certain casualness, a measure of spontaneity, an air of adventure, an *anything-is-possible* quality: a with-itness. He is tall enough that we will see him as masculine, but not so tall as to tower over others, because *Who would want a protagonist who literally looks down on them?* — say, six-one.

Dashiell knows a few things about his name. It is French in origin, originally *De Chiel*, and means, depending upon one's source, *memorable*, or *unknown*, or *from the village of Chiel*, and though when he was a boy he was convinced that his parents had given him a girl's name to make his life

that much more difficult, it was, in fact, an act of naming young Dashiell
after his father, whose own father had been a fan of the American author of
hard-boiled detective fiction, Dashiell Hammett, whose own name was
derived from his mother's surname, and whose work included the likes of
Sam Spade, "The Maltese Falcon," "The Thin Man," et al. But you know
young boys. Dashiell did not want a girl's name, and that was that. At least,
that was that back then. And so he had turned his back on that offending,
feminizing portion of his name, had amputated the -iell, had cut his name in
half. But Dashiell has long outgrown the Dash of old, and now is thankful to
his parents for giving him such a literary name, for, irony heaped upon
irony, Dashiell now writes fiction.

The senior Dashiell had been proud of his son throughout his life, but
found that pride sorely tested when, as they will, the angst-ridden years of
young Dash's teens arrived. This is how it is between fathers and sons:
Conflict is inevitable. Young Dash tried punk rock, but finding that too harsh
a characteristic for a protagonist who we wish to keep sympathetic, decided
on a carefully selected catalogue of lesser-known but critically applauded
alternative rock bands. It was all part of young Dash's rebellion against the
central authority figure in his life: His father. This is how it is between
fathers and sons.

Here is Dashiell: In a flashback to the final straw, we see the son railing against an unwanted intrusion into his life by the father, who has informed our protagonist that the father disapproves of young Dash's girlfriend, despite the length of their relationship, despite said length standing in testament to the strength of said relationship, the father tells the son that he does not see in the boy that fire sparked by True Love, and tells the son that he would not want the boy to make the mistakes that he, the father, has made, a revelation that both insults young Dash's sense of his own manhood and adulthood and self-governance, and lets slip that the father has never been truly in love with young Dash's mother.

Unforgiveable.

In a declaration of his own manhood and adulthood and the rest, young Dash accuses his father of having lived a lie for all of young Dash's 25 years, and more. Recall that this is a flashback. Young Dash had become more confident in his masculinity and less wary of challenges to it, and he'd been thinking about reclaiming the -iell half of his name anyway.

Communication between father and son becomes strained. The two are scarcely on speaking terms.

A brief meditation on the intervening years, the time at graduate school, learning that his undergrad degree hadn't taught him much of anything, earning the graduate degree in writing, knowing that that was an insane expenditure of time and money, but that, damn it, he wanted to

write. The first gray sneaking into the now-close-shorn sides of his hair. The

years spent with Claire, whose real name is Eclair, and who strongly

suspected her own parents of naming her after a pastry, and whose slender

frame, not too slender, and vibrant and long and red hair, and whose

dramatically feminine swoops and curves Dashiell loves to sketch in charcoal

on newsprint — their house is littered with said sketches — and who adored

Dashiell more than she ever thought she would adore anyone when another

man, Dashiell's father, disapproved of her and Dashiell stuck by her, chose

her over his own father. And yes, graduate school had been a rougher ride

without the fiscal support of his parents, but that fact had been liberating,

and they had done it together, had Dashiell and Clair, had worked together

to prove to the father and the world that the two of them could do anything

together, had blazed their own path, seeing the father, who now broods on

the page as a bitter, aging man, back at Dashiell's childhood home in Iowa

only on the major holidays, flying back from California, where they had

made their way, and through the years, so few words exchanged between

the father and the son not only because of the son's anger at the father's

revelation that he did not love the mother, but because, knowing that,

Dashiell could not even reveal to his own mother why he was so very angry

with the father without also causing her grievous emotional injury. And so

the father, as one might guess, as, in fact, you might guess, had become more and more withdrawn with each visit, and Dashiell, the son, angry, honestly did not mind much at all.

His decision to be known, now, as Dashiell, rather than *Dash*, his reclamation of the portion of his name that he had denied, not only doubles the weight of his name from four letters to eight, but also provides us, the readers, with a symbolic transition from boyhood to manhood, though we understand that certain trials, certain tests, must be played out before we agree that he has earned said claim, to wit:

- The brief break-up that tested Dashiell's relationship with Claire, during which both tested the waters in what were ultimately unsatisfying flings, flings which convinced the two to give their relationship another chance, and which ultimately made their bond stronger; and:

- The painful decision to maintain contact with Dashiell's parents principally through commercially purchased greeting cards, tersely filled, on birthdays, holidays, and the worst: Father's Day; and:

- Because no protagonist should be *Dudley-Do-Right* flawless, the fling, the disastrously stupid and unthinkable fling with the undergrad at his graduate institution, and his guilt and his

sorrow, and the love he shares with Claire mending things
slowly, painstakingly, with time; and:

- The financial troubles that arose when both attempted to attend
graduate school, and the decision in which, ultimately, they
decided to take turns — he would work as a newspaper copy
editor while she attended, then she would take a job designing
documents for a business printing company through his
schooling.

It all required maturity and sacrifice from both.

And the love, the True Love, that Dashiell felt for Claire, but secretly
suspected said love to be built at least partly upon the crushing desire to
prove his father wrong, a suspicion Dashiell could not even admit to himself,
lest the whole thing come down like a house of cards.

And then the phone call, late enough that at first the lateness of it
irritates Dashiell and Claire, then, because only drunkenly-dialed wrong
numbers or messages of bad news arrive in this manner and at this hour, so
around 2:30 am, say, the phone call where Caller ID lets us know in advance
that the call is from Iowa, from home, from his parents' telephone, and we
hesitate, because bad news from home at this hour is bad news from home
at this hour.

We have nearly caught up with the present: Dashiell and Claire are in their mid-thirties, and the father and mother are getting older, not so spry and vital as they had been those nearly 10 years back, when the father made the revelation that sent the son away so full of rage. In the intervening years, two novels, critically well-received, have fired forth from the literary cannon of Dashiell's writing cabin, the tiny cabin in the wooded rear of their home, which he has wall-papered with encouraging rejections from major publishers, alongside two acceptances from a small, respectable literary press, so the prestige arrived without much money to back it up. But the phone call: The mother's voice, on the line from Iowa, tells Dashiell what we all sensed was coming: Dashiell's father has died. And Dashiell realizes that he's barely spoken with the man these past ten, and, to his horror, realizes also that he had unconsciously assumed that he still had time to somehow, however unlikely the situation or the odds, somehow patch things up with the old man, but that now such a resolution could never happen.

And we see through his actions — reassuring the mother, flying home to Iowa to oversee the funereal details, never mentioning the feud with the father once, not once — that Dashiell is indeed no longer the boyish young man who'd shortened his name for flare and to reduce challenges to his masculinity, that he is, indeed, a man now, and seeing to manly affairs, no matter how painful they might be. Indeed, Dashiell now realizes just how puerile and absurd the notion of calling oneself *Dash* really was, realizes: *I was that afraid of the judgment of others.*

But the scene that we almost flew past as we approached the end of the tale was this, which took place immediately after Dashiell and Claire arrived at the parents' home:

Dashiell: "Mom, I'll understand if you can't talk about it, but it's important to me to know. How did he die?"

Mother, tears welling: "He'd withdrawn quite a bit over the past few years, quite a bit. He changed his office, you know. Not right after you left — but eventually."

And the mother leads her grown son to the father's office to find dozens of favorable reviews of Dashiell's stories and novels framed and hung — indeed, entire hardcover editions of both of the son's novels have been mounted and framed and encased and hung here, the father's office transformed into a shrine honoring the son.

Mother, voice wavering: "You were an unexpected child, Dashiell, but we made do, maybe even married too soon at the news. He died here, communing with you as best he could."

And we know without them speaking the words that the old man had loved Dashiell, that, despite the fact that the official cause of death was *myocardial infarction* and despite the risk of it coming off as corny, this story has built up enough currency by this point that it might just get away with communicating to us, in this manner, that the father had, in fact, died of a

broken heart. And in light of these new details, we see the father, far from

the sort of indifferent, unloving monster his son had thought him to be,

revealed instead as the pained and tragic figure the father actually was.

And that nagging suspicion that our protagonist would not face: That

possibility that he loved Claire so fiercely specifically to prove his father

wrong, we understand that he must face that, no matter what penalty and

danger facing such a thing might bring because, well, the reader needs to

know. So Dashiell confronts said suspicion, knowing that if it is true, then his

life has run parallel with his father's, and he, Dashiell, has loved falsely,

which means that he would take his place transposed with his father in the

position of said tragic figure, actually *become* said tragic figure. But the

narrator has mercy: This is not such a story. Dashiell confronts the

suspicion, recalls all he and Claire have accomplished through the years, and

in a Chekhovian moment, confronts his own reflection in the mirror and

gives himself, as we say, a hard look. And he decides that his fear was just

that: merely an insecurity, a secret worry to be cast out, purged as one

purges demons, now, put behind them, forgotten. He and Claire have a

maturity and a commitment and, yes, a True Love, which they will need with

the baby boy on the way.

And we understand this because this is how it is between fathers and

sons.

Jønathan Lyons's writing has appeared in *Hotel Amerika, Phoebe, Pank, The Journal of Experimental Fiction,* and other literary journals, and been included in several anthologies. His work has twice been nominated for Pushcart Prizes. He also serves as an essayist and affiliate scholar for the Institute for Ethics and Emerging Technologies.

www.ingramcontent.com/pod-product-compliance
Lightning Source LLC
Chambersburg PA
CBHW060625130626
46555CB00002B/666